Clit Notes

A SAPPHIC SAMPLER

Grove Press
New York

Clit Notes

A SAPPHIC SAMPLER

by Holly Hughes

Published simultaneously in Canada
Printed in the United States of America

Library of Congress Cataloging-in-Publication Data
Hughes, Holly.
    Clit notes: a Sapphic sampler / by Holly Hughes. — 1st ed.
        p.   cm.
    Contents: The well of horniness — The lady dick — Dress suits to
hire — World without end — Clit notes.
    ISBN 0-8021-3333-9
    1. Lesbians—Drama.   2. Monologues.   I. Title.
PS3558.U368C58   1996   813' .54—dc20   95-39497

DESIGN BY LAURA HAMMOND HOUGH

Grove Press
841 Broadway
New York, NY 10003

02 03 04 05   10 9 8 7 6 5 4 3

To the WOW Cafe,

which got me started,

and to Esther Newton,

who keeps me going.

Contents

Introduction

've been invited here to talk to you about my work. And I'm starting to panic because I don't think I can do what I've been asked to do. I'm not sure I can come up with a dozen pages of thespian anecdote peppered with theory. I'm afraid you're going to want to read all about my formal innovations, and you'll look for details about my process. This is what folks usually want to know when they ask about my work.

I hope you don't mind if I decide to perform rather than write this introduction. If I can pull off this performance, then maybe I can change this book from a piece of writing into a quiet room where we can *talk* and have a little show and tell.

I want my work to be like the small glass tumbler I'm clutching in my sweaty hand; unremarkable but important because it holds something I need. So this is what I want to talk to you about, not the structure of the work, but what I put inside it. I like performance art for the same reason my mother's bridge club was crazy for Tupperware; it's a good container, sturdy, nothing too fancy. I want to fill my work with something as clear and necessary as cold water; then I want to give it away. Of course, it'll be water from my well, warmed by the heat of my body, and it'll taste like me.

I don't pretend what I'm doing is new. I tell stories whose shapes are familiar to anyone lucky as I was to be showered with stories earlier. When I talk about my work, I'm always afraid that I'll be dismissed because I'm likely to be outside of anyone's definition of the avant-garde. I want people to love what I do for the reason I do: it isn't new. I didn't invent it. Nobody owns it. I want to point out the signs of wear and tear that prove it's been used. I want to answer those who yawn, "It's been done," by saying: "Yes." And it will be, again and again. Like sleeping, eating, dreaming. Done because of some need, a craving to tell a story, that's balanced by a hunger to listen.

Was telling stories the first distinctly human thing we did?

When I get lucky, when the performance works, the audience stops worrying about my form and forgives me for using something that doesn't belong to me. If I'm really lucky, they're able to use what pours out of these words. Sometimes they even like what I want to give them. And if not, there's always that chance they could acquire a taste.

I'm hoping that here with you in this room, this space some people might call a book, that I'll have one of those lucky breaks when I don't have a script, but what I wanted to have happen is happening. I'm thinking out loud; I'm writing with my body. I don't feel like I'm doing something; it feels as though I'm not stopping something from happening. For a few moments the words are coming out as easily and thoughtlessly as breath. I'm telling stories about how I became an artist and how I became a lesbian. And the different stories are all leading in the same direction, right towards the place I want to go, into that tangled and unmapped thicket where life and art meet.

"I wouldn't be an artist if I weren't a lesbian," I say. I tell whoever's in the room that I can't separate one desire from another; my love for words and my love for women flowing from the same place inside me. This is where I go to get the water I promised you.

Suddenly I realize I have no idea what I'm talking about!

I'm lost. I ask myself: Why didn't I make a map? I could have stayed on the path I made, saying what I've said before.

But I wanted to go some place new.

All I can think is: thank God, I've got an audience. At least one pair of eyes are on me as I stumble through the story (stories) of my life (lives). And they're paying attention. I can tell they're following me, even though I'm plainly lost, because there's a light shining out of their eyes. I make my way along in this light, knowing I'm being watched. Not in an Orwellian sort of way but watched in the sense of being watched over, guarded.

Having an audience is a form of protection. It's like having the light of a hundred tiny private suns helping me find my way from one side of the story to the next.

What does my audience get from this? What's in it for them? Can't be sure. I take the light to mean my work is working for them, and I hope it'll work for you in some way. There's something I want to give you, something I hope you can use. Of course, I'm never sure how it'll be used, and there's always that chance that what is found here will be used against me. Still I know I need the light of your eyes on me. I never would have found this place without you. Thank you for coming. I need to be watched like this. I couldn't do this on my own.

When I was nine the doctors told me I could have a normal life.

If I wanted.

My parents brought me on the recommendation of the school principal. I had been sent to her office for refusing to outline everything I drew in black crayon. She had asked me if I could not see the black line around everything. There were other problems, for example, my habit of stealing my father's *Playboy* and reading it under my parents' bed. My father only had one issue, which is all you really need if it's a really good one, and I guess his was, because he didn't feel much like sharing his *Playboy* with his daugther. Both my teachers and parents worried that I was too expressive; not only did I talk too much but I used my body too much when I talked. I remember my parents telling the doctors they worried that the way I spoke made me look "ethnic."

And, of course, we weren't. My mother's family hadn't been ethnic in hundreds, possibly thousands of years. My father had a few drops of ethnic in him, but he had learned to dress so no one could guess he or anyone he ever met was the least bit ethnic.

The doctors my parents took me to see were specialists. Three orthopedists and a proctologist. They made me walk around the office naked for an hour; then they had a conference with my parents and me. Yes, there was something wrong with me, and it was particularly evident when I took all my clothes off. My father wanted a diagnosis, but the doctors encouraged us to look on the bright side. Why dwell on the fact that I was not and would never be normal when I could still have a perfectly normal life? My parents should realize how common my problem was. The doctors assured them that even if I was abnormal, at least I wasn't unusual, and they went on to add we would be surprised to know how many people were not normal but appeared to be, because they had chosen to have completely normal lives.

It's the mid-sixties but not where I am. The sixties won't happen in my hometown until 1979, and then they will only take the form of a single head shop next to the downtown J. C. Penney. I'm white and middle class, but then who isn't? No one I know. Being white and middle class, it's like having two eyes and two legs. It's normal.

I'm living in a part of the country most people fly over on the way to someplace else. The most distinctive feature of the landscape is the wide river that runs through it and divides the country in at least two. It's a river of silence. What the river looks like depends on where you're standing. I was born on one side, where silence is golden, where answering "How are you?" by saying anything other than "Fine!" is as unthinkable as screaming: "Fire!" in a crowded theater. Somehow I've crossed over to the side of the river where silence equals death.

It's at this moment in the doctors' office that my life in theater really starts. Their diagnosis gives my life a shape, turns it into a story; at the doctors' words I stop living my life and start acting out a drama. Like any drama it's driven by conflict; in this case, the conflict between the two central characters and their irreconcilable desires.

I get to play both characters. I am the woman who will do anything to have a normal life, and I am also the one who gets in her way, who wants something for which she has no name. I play the part of the one who carefully outlines everything in black, keeps everything separate and contained, and I also play the part of the woman who never met a line she wouldn't cross, who is continually going out of bounds. I am the woman who is still trying to digest the patty-melt luncheon I attended after winning the Kiwanis Club Good Citizenship Award; I am also the dyke that Donald Wildmon claimed was using federal money to make child pornography.

Everything is weighted in favor of the former; including the language in which this story is being told. Just as everything in French is divided into one of two categories, male or female, everything in the language of the place I was born is divided into the normal and the not normal. I know what normal looks like. I know what the doctors are saying is that I could grow up to become my parents. I could have a life with two new cars, two children, a two-story house, and I could be one of two people in a marriage as full of resentment as our Frigidaire is full of condiments.

What I don't know is what the not normal looks like. In my first language the abnormal doesn't require a different article. It just disappears. So I learn to speak a language full of holes, riddled by the unspeakable. I'm full of questions about the life I've been taught to call normal, but I don't know how to put these questions into words. I don't have any ways to describe the kind of life that something inside me seems to want; I simply can't imagine becoming something other than my parents. Instead I try to find myself through a variety of methods: bowling, Christianity, calligraphy, crash diets, and macramé, to mention only a few. Although none of these activities provided much enlightenment, all were quite helpful in realizing another important goal of mine: irritating my parents.

They are of course major players in the little drama of my life. My parents play supporting roles; that is, they try to support my ambitions to be normal. My mother hangs her wedding dress in the bedroom closet. At night I hear it scratching to get out and swallow me whole. When I sleep, I dream my parents' dreams. Every day I wake up to find my body looking less and less familiar, less like my body and more like my mother's.

But sometimes their methods backfire. One summer they send me to a camp that promises to turn me into a Christian leader by improving my golf game. On the first day, right after breakfast, we are herded off for forty-five minutes of Christian Ideals, the first of the day's many religious activities. My teacher is a woman named Buddy. I had never seen a woman who looked like Buddy, although I had seen a few men who did, but only in my dreams. She began by asking us if we knew where our vaginas were. Buddy warned us we'd never survive five weeks at camp if we insisted on using Kotex. Learning how to insert a tampon was the first Christian ideal we put into practice.

Buddy realized most of us had no idea where the tampon should go. All I knew was that my vagina was probably in one of two places. Possibly it was in a safety-deposit box sitting on top of the fifty-dollar savings bond that my Uncle Red gave me when I was born. Other times, when my mother described my vagina as a beautiful gift I would give my husband, I thought: "So that's what's all wrapped up and collecting dust under my bed!" I wondered if my parents had gotten it at Sears or J. C. Penney. I hoped my husband would know how to put the beautiful gift together, because I sure didn't, and I hoped he would give me something really good, too.

The entire camp was run by women like Buddy, women with names like Horace, Killer, B.J., Billy, and, of course, Butch. These are not the kind of names somebody can give you; you have to *earn* them. Which these women did, usually by helping out tenderfoot campers like *moi*, young women who were forever losing their vaginas somewhere in the deep woods and always needed a hand to find them again.

My parents visit, but somehow they fail to notice that the place they've sent my sister and me to is not the Christian leadership camp they thought it would be but a big dyke training ground. When I come home, my parents want to know what I've learned, and so I give a little recitation, not of the Bible verses I had expected to study but the little bouquet of haiku I penned for Buddy. My parents listen appreciatively, and they act as if nothing is wrong, but the part of me that wants to be normal knows better. On the drive home my mother talks about what was so great about Marilyn Monroe. Both men and women liked her, she says, and in case I missed the point she adds that she often thought the way she felt about her was "unnatural."

Suddenly I can see the line, and I can see that my mother has crossed over it, and now I am standing in the place that's tight and neat, all filled in, and my mother is standing somewhere outside where everything gets blurry; she's speaking to me from the place where my words won't go. I feel like calling up the proctologist and my school principal, and turning my parents in. For five years in a row my parents send me off each summer to learn how to be a lesbian, and I start to wonder if this is my drama or theirs—I'm not quite sure what's being acted out.

Then there were the semiannual family outings to the local art museum, where my parents warned my sister and me we would be "exposed" to art. The permanent collection consisted entirely of postcards someone had brought back from Europe. An hour away is another museum with actual paintings, but we never go; my parents don't want us to die of exposure.

I couldn't figure out how looking at art was going to help me have a normal life. First of all, the subject of most of the pictures in the museum was the same as in *Playboy*—naked bodies, mostly women. What made some pictures dirty and some pictures art? How was I supposed to look at this stuff? I decided to look at art the way the doctors had looked at me. I tried to guess which of the naked women were normal and which were not, which had the best shot at having a normal life.

The trips were my mother's idea, and I would think she would have known better. After all, she had an artistic side, something we talked about in the same way we talked about the family's tendency to have high blood pressure, flatulence, and melanomas. Creativity was a disfiguring if not fatal affliction, and my mother had to constantly struggle against her tendency to express herself. In the museum my mother made my sister and me hold her hands. She wasn't worried that we might damage the art, but she knew that art could damage us. People, especially women, of our milieu were not supposed to have selves, and if they did, they were expected to keep them tied up in the backyard.

My mother self-medicated her creativity away through shop therapy. She bought art. Making art was not normal, but buying it was. In fact, you could make almost anything normal by buying it. My mother collected reproductions of folk art. Then she would try to copy the reproduction. The end result, the copy of the copy, she would consider an "original," making my mother perhaps the first postmodern north of Toledo. We could have afforded the real thing, but we were so middle class we didn't know any folk, nor did we have any intention of knowing any folk in the future. In fact, other than shopping, my family's major creative outlet consisted of maintaining as much distance as possible between ourselves and anyone that might be considered folk.

Fast-forward to 1973. I'm in college. New languages are coming out of the civil rights, antiwar, and women's movements. But I don't know anyone who speaks these languages. The world is changing but not my world. I'm in a small Midwestern town, trapped in the normal. I want out, but I don't know how to get there from here. Getting out has something to do with language. If I had the right words, I thought, I could talk myself out. In the meantime I read poetry.

My favorite poet comes to the college, a man famous for his bear poems. I'm sure this man is going to say something that will change my life. But when the question-and-answer period comes, I don't know how to put my question into words. I ask the poet what the bears in his work mean. But what I really want to know is, where did the bear come from?

I knew it came from somewhere inside him, inside his body, and that's what made the poems so good. But how could you locate the place in your body where words lived? My body was still a foreign country, still occupied by my parents, the doctors, the storm troopers of the normal. Maybe if he told me how he found his bear, something in his story would help me reclaim my body, would open my heart so language could move through me, so the words could come out. This is what I wanted to ask the poet but didn't know how: tell me a story.

Now I am an artist who makes part of her living doing performances followed by question-and-answer periods. A lot of the questions I'm asked are about sex and gender, about privilege and power, about who gets to speak and who has to listen. I try to entertain rather than answer these questions. That is, I encourage the audience to live with these questions, to resist the epidemic of easy answers.

I know these people expect me to tell them the truth, and the truth is fine for some people, but a lot of us need more. We need a story. There's often a question beneath the questions I'm being asked, and most of the time it's this: *tell me a story.* How did I get from there to here. "There" meaning the comfortable trap of middle-class life with its culture of silence and amnesnia. "Here" being someplace not yet charted, off center, marginal but offering more room to maneuver. They want a map, a set of directions saying "This way out."

Of course, they'll have to make their own maps. But something in my story might help them with theirs. They might begin to think of their own life as a story, might realize they can write this story, that they can be the heroine, that they can create their own plot rather than to go on living inside the standard narrative. Of course, maybe the stories I'll give them won't work for them in the way I hoped, but I'm sure they can find some use for them. As far as I can tell, everyone can always use a story.

It was my parents who taught me how to imagine a life different from theirs. They gave me stories.

Every night my sister and I would beg: "We need a story." One of my parents, generally my mother, would give us what we wanted: a fairy tale read from a battered brown book. We liked to hear the same stories over and over, and luckily, my mother took requests. I didn't ask for them by name, and it wasn't the plot I wanted to revisit; I wanted the images. I wanted to hear again and again about the white snake, the blue light at the bottom of the well, and about all the plants and animals that were silent in my world but in these stories spoke. I was willing to endure a lot of happily-ever-afters to get what I needed.

It was almost always my mother who read to us, because my father was where he always was, somewhere else, gone. When we asked her where he was, my mother rarely gave us a simple answer. She didn't just say he had to go back to work, or he's out playing golf. She'd take these details and expand on them; in short, she'd give us a story, usually one that built upon the elements of the fairy tales she read to us. But the ones she made up were never as good as the ones in the book, or at least I didn't like them as well because hers were always short on magic and long on plot.

My mother used the same story for every occasion, whether it was my father's absence or explaining why she didn't want me to hang out with kids from the working-class neighborhood that bordered on ours. In the story my mother was making up about our lives, the one she gave my sister and I before we slept to shape our dreams, my father was a kind of king, and she was, of course, the queen. She wanted us to believe we were living in the happily-ever-after, but her story didn't hold water: it couldn't explain away my father's continued absence or account for her own apparent depression.

Anyway I didn't want to be a princess. I'd rather be the talking flower, the blue light in the well, the path through the dark woods. I wondered what would happen if I let the wolf get me. What if I'd rather be eaten than rescued?

I began to make up my own stories. Different plots began to occur to me. My parents and teachers began to accuse me of not being in touch with reality. Of course, they were right. And I must say that losing touch with reality at such an early age was the best thing I ever did for myself. As you'll see in this tome, the low opinion of reality I formed so early in my life has not improved. I am convinced that it was only my ability to detach from reality that got me through my childhood.

I started to get the feeling that this reality everybody wanted me to get in touch with was just another set of stories. The stuff I was trying to learn at school and the things my mother was telling me at home started to sound like two parts of the same fairy tale. Even though the sixties were not happening in the place where I was living, we could catch glimpses of them, or rather we couldn't avoid watching Detroit, less than a hundred miles away, burn; but we did not talk about them.

As we watched, I wondered why all the stories I was hearing seemed designed to make me go to sleep.

On weekends we made pilgrimages to northern Michigan, rarely speaking for most of the three-hour trip, and I thought to myself: *This is not a family. This is a Buick containing four individually wrapped slices of American cheese.* Once in a while I'd break up the silence by begging my parents to take us to visit the Amazing Mystery Spot, where billboards promised we could witness phenomena that defied the laws of nature. I had no idea what the laws of nature were, but I didn't let that stop me from wanting to defy them. My parents complained that the mystery spot was too far off the beaten path, which sounded to me like just another reason to go.

I refused to believe I had sprung from the loins of people whose worst nightmare was of taking a wrong turn, who were always in a big hurry to get nowhere, so I told myself that these people were not my real family. Sooner or later, my real family would come back for me. I would know them when I saw them, and the first thing we'd do together would be to visit the mystery spot. In the back of the car I invented a new family, imagining us traveling to the place that was almost off the map, standing together somewhere where we could see how everything could be different.

Stories could also carry me into the future, which I was convinced would be another country. I pretended what was happening around me was a series of flashbacks in a TV show where I was the star. When my mother descended on me wearing just a black panty girdle and matching rage, I reminded myself I couldn't be killed off: *without me there could be no story.* Awakened by my parents fighting, I'd slide into the future where my stories had made me so famous I had a slot on the *Hollywood Squares,* and where my family were jokes I was trying out on Paul Lynde, my best friend.

But being famous meant more than just getting to hang with the likes of Charo, Nipsy Russell, and Rose Marie. Being famous meant your words had weight. What you said became more than just a story. If you were famous, whatever you said was the truth.

Stories gave me exactly what I wanted; they opened places for me to disappear, where no one could follow. After years of watching my life from the outside, of getting through the day by telling myself, "It's only a movie," I wanted something else. It gets lonely being invisible. I wondered if I could make words work in another way, if they could open as well as shut doors.

I came to Manhattan to take classes at the New York Feminist Art Institute, with the hopes that all my aesthetic, political, and sexual goals could be conveniently met under one roof. All in all, I found the transition from born-again bowler to feminist fairly smooth. It was 1979, the salad days of the movement. I left Michigan with visions of all the sisterly, nonhierarchical art we were going make. We were gonna topple the patriarchy by scattering huge sculptures of vaginas around public spaces and by renaming ourselves after our mothers' favorite condiments or obscure appliances found in the attics of famous women of the past.

This was the plan, at least. For the most part these theories went untested. Unfortunately, by the time we students arrived at the collectively run institute, most of the members of the collective were no longer speaking to each other.

Within six months my painting was in remission. Most of the students who weren't from New York went back to wherever it was they came from. I stayed put, but I was still doing what I had done back in the mitten state. I was a waitress without a cause. Between shifts, I strolled through SoHo, frustrated by what I saw. Minimalism just didn't do the trick for me. I've never been able to convince myself less is more. I had a teacher who had talked about how she liked to slip inside paintings whenever she could. I remember her describing what happened when she saw an Ellsworth Kelly painting for the first time. The whole canvas opened up, and she walked inside it, into a world of blue.

I wanted that to happen to me. I wanted to slough off my uniform redolent of London broil and yesterday's coleslaw, and walk into this other world, a place where words would fail me, where color and light would speak. At night I rolled quarters as I read *Art Forum*, hoping to learn the magic words that would make art open for me.

But when the art did speak, I heard a voice from an old, not new, world. I heard the voices of the Protestant suburbs, the voices of my parents—all trying to convince me that less is more. I saw a Carl Andre installation, rows of bricks on an oak floor and thought: "Well, Carl, that's a nice start, but now what are you going to do with it?" For a minute I couldn't remember where I was—Paula Cooper Gallery or a Color Tile outlet?

In another gallery I saw paintings of enlarged wallpaper. This work was not less, but neither was it more. I kept on believing that art could show me a way out of the past, but all this art seemed to be leading me backwards, reminding me of easy-care fabrics, of one-stop shopping, and Hamburger Helper, of people in a big hurry to go nowhere. I looked at this art and said to myself, under my breath: "No. Less is just less. Only more is more."

I was having even less luck in bed than I was having in the studio. (Of course, I didn't have a studio, which may have been part of the problem, but I digress.) Sometime during the dawn of the Carter administration, I had looked at another woman, and I felt towards her the way I imagine calf's liver must feel towards fried onions. That is, I needed to get her on top of me to feel complete. (I launched my careers as a lesbian and as a waitress simultaneously, and find I'm still prone to conflate the culinary and the sapphic.)

I assumed that wanting to have sex with women meant I was a lesbian, so I went looking for other lesbians who I hoped would show me the ropes, so to speak. I did find dykes who were only too willing to set me straight. What made somebody a lesbian, I was told, wasn't wanting to have sex with women; it was wanting to get away from men. In fact, if you admitted you wanted to have sex with women, you would be accused of being just like a man; it was the very worst thing you could do. Apparently, sex was something lesbians used to do before they got politics and opened food co-ops. Desire was a thing of the past, a world that these dykes had rejected as unequivocally as I had that of my parents. As for theater, I never touched the stuff until I was hopelessly lost.

In 1982, I see a sign advertising Double X-rated Christmas Party for Women. I'm there as soon as the doors open. Racks of thrift-store tuxedos and prom dresses by the coat check encouraged you to slip into something not necessarily more comfortable but definitely more festive. Inside, all sorts of women were carrying on. There were kissing booths. Strip shows. One of the drag queens selling drinks told me what I was seeing was WOW. The women looked somehow familiar. But I didn't know them from the food co-op. I had seen them twice before. Most recently I had seen them in photographs of dyke life before lesbian feminism. Butches and femmes. The kind of lesbians that supposedly died out in the seventies.

But the first place I had seen these women was in my own dreams, in the stories I had made up to get me through childhood. This was the family I'd dreamed, my real family. And here we were together, right in the place I knew we would be. WOW was the place I'd always wanted to visit—the mysterious *mystery spot*. Here we were invisible from the beaten path. Going too far was the only way to go. WOW was a place where transformation was possible, where women came to be changed. A place where every moment began with the determination to defy the laws of nature.

In 1983, WOW found a permanent home, a tiny linguini-shaped storefront on East Eleventh, where it only takes three people to make a crowd scene. I don't know who I am yet—I'm not a performance artist—nevertheless, I am determined to express myself. I'm sure that here at WOW I'll be able to develop a self worth expressing. WOW isn't sure who she is yet, either. There are a few rules, but breaking them is not only tolerated, it's almost encouraged. After all, we advertise ourselves as a home for wayward girls. Most of us were refu-

gees from lesbian feminism who had gone AWOL from other collec-
tives. WOW was safe not only from the male gaze but also from a feminism convulsed by the sex wars. No one had to reclaim butch and
femme; no one there had renounced it. No one worried about losing
funding; no one got any. We had jobs. If we were lucky. Here, the fights
were over whether we should get a pool table or a piano.

Lois Weaver of the Split Britches trio teaches a weekly acting
class that almost everyone in WOW attends, regardless of their thespian aspirations. Performance happens almost by accident, as by-
products of the theme parties we have to throw monthly to pay the
rent. There's nobody to say you weren't good enough or weren't right
for the part. There's nobody to say no. Just work the door a few times
and you can have your own show, which we assumed was what everyone wanted. Our assumption was you came to WOW looking for two
things: pussy and a place to perform. (I borrow from Minnie Bruce Pratt
for my new definition of what it means to be a lesbian: she's a ham, a
woman who'll perform at the drop of a hat.)

I began making theater in 1983. The kind of theater I make is
generally and often pejoratively called performance art. Like any form
of theater, performance art involves creating your own reality and then
somehow forcing a bunch of other people to sit through it. From my
experience it seems the principal difference between theater and performance art is head shots.

Also, theater and performance art often occur in different
places. Theater tends to happen in theaters, whereas performance art
tends to happen in spaces. A theater will be defined for the purposes
of this piece as somewhere with a stage, some lights, a box office, a
dressing room, head shots, and people who know how to run these
things. A theater is a place that has been designed for theater, whereas
a space has been designed for some other purpose: it's a gas station, an
art gallery, somebody's living room, a church basement, and it's almost always better suited for pancake suppers and giving oil changes
than for performing. There is a BYO ethos at work in spaces: bring

your own chairs, lights, stage, toilet paper. If such appliances are available at the performance space, there will either be no one who knows how to run them or someone who is so badly paid they refuse to do so. If there is no money in American theater, there is even less in performance art. Because it is a poor art form, performance art is often made and watched by the kinds of people who rarely get to make theater.

WOW is a space even though it has some accoutrements of a theater. For example, WOW has sound and lighting equipment that would have made it a state-of-the-art theater in postwar Bulgaria. One can also find people at WOW who know how to coax these antiques into service, and who will gladly do so if you only help them with their productions. Sexual favors are not required, nor are they refused.

My artistic motivations and process were evident early. My primary motive for doing what I do was and remains meeting girls. I cannot blame lesbian feminism entirely for the sorry state of my sex life prior to discovering WOW. The truth is I had no valuable lesbian skills. Sports, particularly those that depend on flying objects, are anathema to me. I have always been openly, though not unequivocally, carnivorous. I can read horoscopes a bit, which is not to say that I know anything about astrology, only that I am willing to look at a piece of paper covered with completely unfamiliar symbols and take a wild guess as to what they may mean. All this changed after I came out as a thespian. When I would get a crush on a girl, I would sit down and write her a play. Then I would cast the beloved in a starring role and would then cast myself as her love object. I tried to script the romances I wanted to have, finding that sometimes life did in fact imitate art.

I stumbled upon my preferred method of working while creating my first major opus. Footnote: I found myself bragging to a couple of women at WOW that I had written quite a bit of pornography with an old girlfriend. This was nothing short of a bald-faced lie. I had done neither the writing nor the girl. Before I knew it I was agreeing to write the screenplay for a lesbian porn movie that these women promised to produce.

So I holed up in my apartment and tried to come up with a title, convinced that once I had the right title the rest of the writing would be downhill. Now I know better, of course. The most important part of a successful production is the poster. Now I work backwards from the flyer. This is the kind of knowledge that one can gain only through experience.

But coming up with a poster or a title has the same requirement. Market research. Who is your audience? What kind of experience do you want them to have? This was easy. My audience was WOW. I'd taken the liberty of promising parts to half the women there, even though I hadn't written a single word. I figured there was a pretty good chance they'd want to see a movie they were in. What emotion did I hope to summon up in my audience? Lust, some of which I hoped might be directed at me.

But the potential producers had a different target audience in mind. Men. They rejected my screenplay as not pornographic enough, that is, it wouldn't turn men on. I thought of tossing the script out, but being ecologically minded I decided to recycle my screenplay as performance art. After all, I had a really good title I didn't want to waste: "The Well of Horniness." (In fact, the title is the best thing about the play, so I repeated it as often as possible.)

When I tried the title out on friends, I got a few appreciative laughs, but mostly what I got was mild disgust. Women, I was reminded, did not get horny; in fact, they couldn't get horny if they wanted to. Didn't I realize that horniness was a word men had invented to describe something that happened only to them? If I really wanted to write about lesbian sexuality, I shouldn't be using the vocabulary of male heterosexuality.

I wasn't sure if I agreed with them. Yes, all right, horniness was a man-made word, but did that mean women never got horny? If that were true, then what did women get? My friends' response was not exactly what I'd been looking for. But it helped me recognize where writing just a few words had taken me. Lesbian desire is a country without a language of its own. If I wanted to chart its terrain, I had two choices: I could use the language of heterosexuality with all its distortions and erasures, or I could use the predominant lesbian dialect of that time, which was a language of shame that trivialized desire. The latter seemed to be no language at all but yet another form of silence.

Women at WOW started making a lesbian theatrical language the same way everyone made all the other things we needed for our shows—sets and costumes. Nobody at WOW could afford anything new. Our prop show was the streets of the East Village. You took what you could find and turned it into what you wanted. The success of your shows depended on your ability to read a pile of garbage and imagine trash translated into theater. Certainly lesbians deserve our own language, not to mention our own wigs. But I continue to look for images in the dumpster of American culture. After *The Well of Horniness* came *The Lady Dick* and then *Clit Notes*. I like taking something someone has thrown away and using it for a purpose for which it was never intended. If a broken kitchen chair could be transformed into a castle, then why not use secondhand language the same way: take it apart, paint it, glue it, pervert its meanings.

WOW's aesthetic was more Charles Ludlam than Jane Chambers; its view of the human condition, more *Gilligan's Island* than *Waiting for Godot*. Although our work was fueled by a variety of ambitions and realized with different levels of skill, there was an unspoken but shared vision of making theater that made community. Some artists hoped to draw an audience from beyond a pool of downtown dykes, but no one made work that tried to convince straight people how nice we were. In fact, a lot of the characters onstage have been stolen from heterosexual nightmares: lesbians as hypersexual, as unrepentant outlaws, vampires, shameless deviants, and perverts.

At WOW I can tell the stories I wanted to hear as a child, short on plot but full of magic. I use words to make a home for myself with passageways that lead from the past into the present. With stories I can dream myself into places I never went, like pre-Stonewall lesbian bar culture or to ground zero of my nuclear family, my parents' bed, where they waged their cold war. In stories new space could be created, places where it is possible to look at what it means to be queer, female, to be white.

By 1986, I started to think about moving what I had built at WOW outside and booked the piece I was writing for Lois Weaver and Peggy Shaw, *Dress Suits to Hire*, at Performance Space 122. Although it's four blocks away from WOW by foot, Performance Space 122 is miles away on the cultural map. That is, it's on the map, whereas WOW is not.

I wanted to work outside of WOW because I wanted to be taken seriously by people who never come to WOW. I didn't plan to change my work, but I wanted to see if I could wrest a few things I'd never be able to get working in the lesbian community, like reviews and maybe a grant. I didn't know what would happen: if the world I built would collapse when I tried to move it, or if the people who found WOW would find me at Performance Space 122. According to lesbian theater scholars, I'd fall victim to the male gaze, meaning my meanings would be perverted, or I'd disappear entirely.

But it's a risk I was willing to take. Increased queer visibility born of the AIDS epidemic made us a better target for right-wing hatred. *They were talking about us.* I thought it was time we stopped talking behind their backs; I wanted to talk back.

When I got the news that John Frohnmayer, then chairman of the National Endowment for the Arts, had vetoed funding for myself and three other performance artists I wasn't the least bit surprised. For at least a year before that, a controversy had swirled around public funding of art that addresses the body, especially the body that's either queer, female, of color, or some combination of those. When Congress passed restrictive language in 1989, equating homosexuality with obscenity, I knew that as one of the few lesbians to get NEA funding for "out" work presented in publicly funded spaces, I was skating on thin ice. So I'd had a year to warm up. I felt ready.

See, this defunding hoopla was supposed to be my big break. Here I was, an artist who spun political parables out of personal experience, caught up in a national debate: hey, *what a great opportunity!* Suddenly I was there in all the papers and on TV, and it seemed to me at first that not only had Frohnmayer's decision given me some great material but it had also dramatically increased the size of my audience overnight. The defunding catapulted me out of the margins right into the mainstream, and I wondered if I shouldn't drop that nice Mr. Frohnmayer a little thank-you note.

Here's what I planned to do. I was going to shape my story into something that could carry all of us—my audience and me—towards other stories, and then I was going to connect all the dots through song, dance, and monologue. I was going to perform my defunding so that my now huge audience would see my story in relation to other stories, like the calls for censorship of rap music, the attacks on sexually explicit AIDS education, and the ongoing struggles over reproductive rights and civil rights. I was sure I could build a time machine into this performance that would let us visit the America of Joe McCarthy, of Anthony Comstock, and of my relatives, the Puritans.

I was no stranger to controversy, and besides, I had performed my way out of some tight spots in the past. There was an anonymous group of D.C. dykes who accused me of being a tool of the heteropatriarchy (their word, not mine), and then there was the prominent expert on queer theater who claimed I couldn't really be a lesbian, because I couldn't speak French. I responded by putting on a pair of high heels and touching up my eyeliner, and when I got through performing, my critics couldn't sit down for a week. (I'm going to let you imagine what that means.) From the time I first tuned out my family by channeling Paul Lynde and Rose Marie, until June of 1990, I'd always been able to find some story that could take me where I wanted to go.

Now I found myself sharing the stage with a whole cast of characters who were either upstaging me or drowning me out. Of course, Jesse Helms, Pat Robertson and Donald Wildmon, and others of their ilk were there all doing their family values and tax-payer waste schtick. Their routines were tired, but they were in the best position to make sure that everybody heard their side of the story. There were several other performances going on as well. The anticensorship movement was doing a big production number designed to save arts funding. But they didn't make a case for the kind of work under attack; either they didn't mention it at all, or they bragged about how few risky grants the NEA had funded. Their performance was an Up with People style revue, complete with marching band, and I was invited to be a part of it as long as I didn't mention why I was there: homophobia.

What kind of show was this anyway? Sometimes I felt like I had landed in the middle of one of those spectacles where a big cultural institution takes a group of artists who have absolutely nothing in common, gives them a bunch of money to collaborate, and then charges the audience an arm and a leg to see the big mess they've made. This is exactly the kind of thing that gives performance art a bad name, and I wanted no part of it.

Other times I felt as though I had become a character in somebody else's drama, Jesse Helms's to be exact, and I couldn't find a way to interrupt his narrative to tell my side of the story. To be sure, I got in a few solos in the form of sound bites. But my story, which was starting to be about death threats and hate mail, about trying to write with the goverment looking over your shoulder, just didn't fit into the fifteen seconds I was alloted.

Meanwhile it looked as if I was losing my audience! Yikes! The people I'd hoped I could talk to—the feminist movement, other political artists, the lesbian and gay communities, intellectuals, and what's left of the left—weren't paying attention to anything that was going on onstage. At best they were snickering at Helms and Co., and heckling me. But most of the audience had stopped watching what was going on onstage; instead, they were arguing among themselves over stuff like which of the NEA Four was truly queer, and whether any of us was good enough to deserve to be defunded. None of the questions they asked each other was about how to counter Jesse Helms; in fact, it was almost as if they had completely forgotten the religious right exists—maybe when the right takes over both houses of Congress, they'll remember.

All of a sudden I don't know who I'm talking to anymore. Is it the group over in that corner who've come looking for a freak show? Should I give them what they've paid for? Or should I be talking to the group over on the left who think that questions of sexuality and culture aren't legitmate political concerns? Is there a way I can perform my story so they'll understand it as a chapter in a much larger story? I don't think there's much I can say to those members of the audience who think any time a member of a traditionally silenced group pipes up they're just whining.

The show keeps running; it's by far the longest performance I've done. Early in the first year I lose my voice. For two years I can't write. But I never leave the stage, knowing if I exit, it'll just make more room for Helms. When my voice comes back, it comes from a deeper place inside me. It has a different tone that comes from recognizing the limitations of words, as well as their power. I can tell that there are some people listening for my voice in the midst of all the other shows that are going on all around me.

This performance has not gone the way I planned. But I have to remind myself of the time I thought I had totally bombed in Kalamazoo. Afterwards a woman approached me, and I took one look at her hair and knew I had nothing to say to her and braced myself for what I was sure she would say to me. Then she told me how much she liked my performance, which she declared the best thing she'd seen since *The Love Boat* had gone off the air!

So I do have an audience after all. I don't know who they are— I can't see all of their faces. I can only hope a few of them are like this woman with hearts as large as their hairstyles. I don't know how they'll use the words I give them. This part of the script isn't finished. My role in the Culture War is still very much a work in progress, a story that I'm telling as I'm living it. But the point is, it needs to be performed in front of an audience. If I'm ever going to be able to write this wrong, I'll need your help.

The Well of
Horniness

The first time a play of mine was published it was recommended that I add some stage directions to the script. I had no idea of how to go about doing that, because none of my work had been performed on a stage at that point. They had been done on a fold couch, on the countertops of a Ukrainian after-hours club, in the kitchen, but never on a stage. How was I to know what somebody should do with these plays onstage?

This play, my first, has never been done the same way twice. One reason for this was we rarely did it in the same place with the same cast twice. The longest run my production of *The Well of Horniness* ever had in New York City was three performances in three different clubs on the same night. I guess that's what I thought they meant by a run: you ran from place to place, trying to make sure you didn't lose any props or cast members along the way.

So I offer the following to be read not as directions so much as serving suggestions. I can describe some of the ways this work was done in the past, but as I said earlier, should you attempt to produce it in a theater you're on your own. I haven't the faintest. Just remember the best thing about *The Well of Horniness* is that it utterly lacks redeeming social value. In the process of writing what I'd hoped would be porn for men, I inadvertently created something for women: an opportunity for us to be silly and wear way too much makeup. Being silly is not the same as being funny, which contrary to popular belief, feminists have always been. But the humor that's come out of the women's movement and the lesbian community is always political; it's useful. Being silly is like taking a vacation from adulthood. So the safest way to do this show might be by going too far and then going a little bit farther.

When this play premiered at the WOW Cafe's first home, that linguini-shaped storefront on East Eleventh Street, the narrator, dressed as a cub reporter and sweating profusely, was downstage left throughout the piece. Other actors entered and exited through a window that led into the adjacent kitchen or into the broken piano we had neglected to remove from the stage. This sounds much more interesting than it actually was.

Those who are put off by my insistence on having only women in the play should note that academic types just can't get enough of this cross-dressing stuff. So it could be your entrée into avant-garde circles, if you don't mind walking in circles.

Part 1 of *The Well* was written several months before the other sections and was originally part of an evening called *Shrimp in a Basket*. The show began with me coming out as a sea captain with a cardboard parrot duct-taped to my shoulder. In a rich mixture of English accents, real and imagined, I welcomed the audience and assured them that if what they were about to see became unnecessarily avant-garde Walkmans would automatically drop from the ceiling; I reminded them that they should put on their own headset before assisting anyone else.

Then I scurried off to WOW's backstage/kitchen area, where I was hot glued into a giant cardboard lobster outfit. This took about twenty minutes and was one of the quicker costume changes of the evening. I'd persuaded a friend to bring the accordion she'd bought that afternoon and entertain the audience with songs of the sea. By the end of the evening, after five or six sets of at least twenty minutes each, what she was playing was starting to sound pretty good, almost like music.

I reemerged with two women also in crustacean drag. We lip-synched to "It Ain't the Meat, It's the Motion," although the audience couldn't tell that's what we were doing, because the lobster suits covered our mouths. The WOW stage was so tiny and the costumes, though exquisite, were so huge and fragile that we couldn't do much more than just stand there while the tape played on a borrowed boom box. Because the tickets for *Shrimp in a Basket* were only $2.99, I think most of the audience felt it was enough for the three of us to just stand in front of them, being big and pink. Then we exited, and it was time for more songs of the sea.

What followed this was a monologue I'd written to showcase the skills for dramatic acting I hadn't bothered to acquire. I tried to compensate by making a big mess that involved potting soil, ketchup, dozens of balloons, and several wigs. All in all, I can say with confidence that the audience was more worried about getting splattered with peat moss than they were with my lack of technique.

The grand finale and hit of what turned out to be a four-hour evening was *The Well of Horniness*, part 1. At first I attributed the piece's popularity to the fact that it was the only part of the evening that had been rehearsed and had anything that could be called a script. But the real secret to the work's success was the talent of the women at WOW, who were willing to use their flesh to flesh out my fantasies.

The piece had another life as a live-radio show produced by Janee Pipik for WBAI in New York City. After that, I began to present the show as a radio play with actors performing all of the sound effects live. This turned out to be quite a crowd pleaser, as well as relieving the cast of the odious task of learning their lines. I have presented this play with as many as ten performers and as few as three. I would not recommend it as a one-woman show, unless that one woman happens to be Sally Field.

The Well had several incarnations in New York City. Somehow I managed to con all of the following into performing at least once, all for free: Peggy Shaw, Maureen Angelos, Carmelita Tropicana, Deb Margolin, Helen Frankenthal, Sally White, Reno, Laura Lanfranci, Sharon Jane Smith, Susan Young, Rebecca High, Robin Epstein, Claire Moed, Ela Troyano, Lisa Kron, Peg Healey, Uzi Parnes, and Lois Weaver.

****

Part 1

NARRATOR: Finally, the story they said couldn't be told shatters the airwaves! Brought to you by House of Shag 'N' Stuff, where tomorrow's carpets are here today, and by Clams A-Go-Go of Passaic, where our motto is: Shellfish Is a Swell Dish! Happy housewives know that when it comes to eating out, nine out of ten men think of one thing.

MAN ONE: Give me fish!

MAN TWO: I want filet!

NARRATOR: And remember! We deliver! When you're thinking of sending something special to that special someone, why not say it with fish!

(*Knock, sound of door opening.*)

WOMAN: Yes?

DELIVERY BOY: Three shrimp dinners!

WOMAN: I didn't order any shrimp dinners . . . this must be somebody's idea of a sick joke!

NARRATOR: Yes! That's exactly right! It's the Well . . .

(*Cast screams.*)

NARRATOR: . . . of Horniness! The continuing saga of one woman's sojourn in the septic tank . . .

(*Toilet flush.*)

NARRATOR: . . . of the soul!

LOUISE: Harold! Come over here! Right this minute!

HAROLD: What is it, Louise?

LOUISE: It's those two new girls on the block, Harold, something about the way they walk, something about the way they talk . . . something about the way they look . . . at each other . . . Harold, I could swear they're Lebanese!

(*Theme from* Twilight Zone.)

HAROLD: You're just imagining things, Louise. They're just a couple of . . . sorority girls.

NARRATOR: Have we got news for you, Harold. Those two girls are members of the Tridelta Tribads, an alleged sorority, but in reality just a thinly veiled entrance to the Well . . .

(*Cast screams.*)

NARRATOR: . . . of Horniness! The setting, a peaceful New England town, just a town like many others, a town that clasped American values to her bosom!

(*Baby crying.*)

NARRATOR: An American town—where every winter day is a White Christmas.

(*Humming "White Christmas."*)

NARRATOR: And every Wednesday night is Prince Spaghetti Night!

OFFSTAGE FEMALE VOICE (*calling*): Anthony!

NARRATOR: Just a town, a town like many others with its local pubs and taverns . . .

(*Cork pop.*)

WAITER'S VOICE: Monsieur, ze Blue Nun, ze 1979!

NARRATOR: . . . and dinner theaters, where tone-deaf emcees flourish, and where the citizens can go to meet, or cheat, that someone special. But beneath the apparently serene breast of new fallen snow a whirlpool rages . . .

(*Sucking noises.*)

NARRATOR: Sucking the weak, the infirm, the original, and all others who don't wear beige down . . . down, down, as carrots in the Cuisinart . . .

(*Sound of a blender.*)

NARRATOR: . . . so are souls in the Well . . .

(*Cast screams.*)

NARRATOR: . . . of Horniness! Meet Georgette.

(*Phone dialing.*)

GEORGETTE: Hello, White Casa? The usual. You know the way I like it —extra hot.

NARRATOR: Coming from one of the town's most established families, her pedigree was unblemished except for a drop of Catholic blood on her mother's side of the family. But underneath the cloak of respectability, evil budded in her bosom. By the time she had pledged her college sorority, Georgette had already fallen into the Well . . .

(*Cast screams.*)

NARRATOR: . . . of Horniness! And Vicki, the town's leading Excedrin consumer!

VICKI: Darn these child-proof tops!

NARRATOR: A recent émigré to this town, like many others she came to this quiet hamlet to forget. By day she clips coupons . . .

(*Sound of scissors.*)

NARRATOR: . . . and attends Aquacise classes. By night she prays for amnesia. Few would guess this well-groomed word-processing trainee was once of the sisterhood of sin. The memories gnaw at her mind like starving hamsters in a Kleenex box.

(*Scratching.*)

NARRATOR: Is there any hope for Vicki? Is there any hope for anyone once they've fallen into the Well . . .

(*Cast screams.*)

NARRATOR: . . . of Horniness! And here's Rod . . .

ROD: Honey, I'm home! Hey, hey, hey, watcha got for me?

(*Glasses clinking.*)

VICKI: I made some Harvey Wallbangers!

NARRATOR: Vicki's fiancé, Georgette's brother, Rod, once had dreams of becoming a golf pro. But like many young men of his milieu, his youthful idealism was trampled by his drive for success. The punch bowl from his graduation open house was barely drained when he became a VP in the family business—a chain of discount carpet warehouses. Rod and Vicki—on the surface just a couple of lovebirds . . .

(*Sound of a kiss.*)

NARRATOR: . . . about to tie the knot!

(*Choking sound.*)

NARRATOR: Then our happy couple makes a date with destiny.

(*Theme from* Jeopardy.)

ROD: Hey, Vick, whaddya say to a little R n' R?

VICKI: Uh, okay.

ROD: Why don't I give my sister, Georgette, a ring? I've been dying for the two of you to meet.

VICKI: Oh, Rod, I really don't feel up to a crowd.

ROD: What's a crowd; she's family. Besides, you'll love her and . . .

(*Snap of fingers.*)

ROD: . . . come to think of it . . . you two were in different chapters of the same sorority!

VICKI: What did you say, dear?

ROD: The same sorority . . . the Tridelta Tribads. Come on, Vick, I remember how you loved that club and those gals!

VICKI: You don't understand; I can never see those women again.

ROD: So who says you have to mention the sorority at all . . . you'll be gabbing about color swatches and floor buffers. Why in no time at all you'll be bosom buddies.

(ROD *starts telephoning* GEORGETTE.)

VICKI: Now I'll never be able to keep the secret of my past from him . . . those so-called sorority sisters!

NARRATOR: Vicki: A would-be word processor with a past she can't outrun!

VICKI: I can't believe his sister is one of *them*! They are . . . everywhere!

NARRATOR: Later that night, Rod and Vicki arrive at the fabulous new dinner theater, The Vixen's Den, where Georgette is already waiting.

BABS: Miss, you're gonna have to check that . . . oh, haven't seen you in a while . . .

GEORGETTE: Oh, hi, how ya doing?

BABS: Since when do you care. Oh, sorry . . . it's just that . . . I thought . . . I mean . . . after we spent . . . together . . . it was special . . .

GEORGETTE: Can it, Babs. I'm here to meet my family. Hey, Babs—who's that foxy lady over by the palms! Whatsa scoop on her?

WAITRESS: Miss, would you like a drink while you're waiting?

VICKI: Uh, I'd like a Harvey Wallbanger. Uh, miss, make it a double.

BABS: I don't know, and I don't care!

GEORGETTE: Yeah, well, I *do*. See ya around, Babs . . .

BABS: Ah, okay, Georgette, call me or I'll call you, okay, Georgette, okay. If I said anything mean about the way we were, I didn't mean it . . .

NARRATOR: Georgette cuts through the dining room as surely as a honey-bee picks out the last wildflower in a field of crabgrass. And where is our hero? There he is: threading his way through the salad bar.

ROD: Pardon me, ma'am, but somebody else might want some croutons, too.

NARRATOR: Will Rod return in time to save his beloved from the predatory clutches of his own flesh and blood? . . . We'll find out after this word from our sponsor . . .

ROD: High cost of wall-to-wall keeping you awake at night? Like to cover up the cement floor in the master bedroom with a little snazzy something or other, but can't shell out an arm or a leg? Then visit New

England's chain of carpet warehouses—House of Shag 'N' Stuff. We're open twenty-four hours to serve you better! Take a look at these beauties! Oh, sorry, we're on the radio. Just listen to these colors! You wouldn't believe how loud they are: *Green!* Red! *Orange!* Yellow! Hot Pink! Yes siree, this week, and this week *only*, we're running a chainwide special on these polytrilon, one hundred percent washable throw rugs in designer colors! Throw 'em anywhere, the kitchen, the living room, throw 'em at the kids . . . heh-heh! Dads! Tired of mowing that big green expanse of nothingness? Got a fortune sunk in weed killer? Pave the whole thing over and just toss around a few of these babies for accent! They'll never notice, and I'll never tell! Once you see our low, low prices and easy terms, you'll be bitten by the bug too! SHAG FEVER! So hurry on down to any one of our convenient locations, or come by our main branch and showroom right off Route Seventeen in this town, a town like many others!

> (VICKI *and* GEORGETTE *are frozen during the monologue,*
> *in near embrace.*)

ROD: Vicki, hon, this is my sister, Georgette. Hey, I'm so glad the two of you, my two favorite gals are finally meeting.

GEORGETTE: So lovely.

VICKI: *Enchantée*, I'm sure.

WAITRESS: The Pasta Arrivederci . . . coming in for a landing.

> (GEORGETTE *starts slurping on noodles.*)

ROD: Georgette! For Chrissakes, this isn't a hamburger joint!

NARRATOR: Despite her resolve, Vicki finds she cannot resist the way Georgette plays with her food.

GEORGETTE: Whatsamatter honey? You sit in a puddle, or you just glad to see me?

WAITRESS: Excuse me, miss, are you gonna order anything, or are you just gonna eat hers?

ROD: Noodles all around, garçonette, and while you're at it, how's about a little fruit of the vine to wash this slop down?

WINE STEWARD: Very well, monsieur! (*Pours wine all over Georgette's blouse.*) Oh, pardon! How clumsy of me.

ROD: Will ya get a load of that! What is it with you guys? Run a wet T-shirt contest on the side?

VICKI: Let me try! Usually if you get it while it's still damp . . .

ROD: Well, whaddya know? It's another testimonial to the miracle of synthetics!

(*Fork falls.*)

NARRATOR: As Vicki's fork clatters to the ground, something darker than etiquette draws Vicki down.

VICKI: Excuse me.

ROD: I suppose I should wait until after dinner, but I really want to pick . . .

NARRATOR: What began innocently enough, takes a turn for the worse underneath the table. Vicki finds no cutlery but Georgette's legs, two succulent rainbows leading to the same pot of gold.

(VICKI *begins to slide underneath the table and slowly
slithers along the floor towards* GEORGETTE.
By the time ROD *mentions Busch Gardens,* VICKI *should
just be getting between Georgette's legs. Let's not rush
things, girls!*)

ROD: . . . your brains on some of the places I've been looking into as possible honeymoon hideaways. I'm looking for something that has a lot to offer, particularly a good golf course. I bought Vick a set of clubs for her last birthday, and darn it all if she doesn't have a better putt than I do! Well, that's neither here nor there. I just mean you can't spend all your time in bed, hah-hah. Right? This South Seas plantation offers a lot—twenty minutes from the Tampa–Saint Pete airport, and ninety minutes from Disney World and Busch Gardens. And Georgette, get a load of this private beach. It's pretty reasonable too, if we take the Americana Plan. The breakfast, the greens' fees, and happy hour are thrown in. Although I must say I'm a bit wary of these all inclusive deals! There's always hidden charges that amount to no savings at all. You gotta be careful, these damned travel agents see the rock on her finger and the stars in my eyes, and they'll soak ya every time, I swear to God, and they'll laugh all the way to the bank, am I right? Well, here's some of the brochures, they all look great on paper. You can take a gander at them after dinner, and Vicki wanted to . . . hey, hey, Vick, what's up? You find that fork yet?

VICKI: I see it, but I can't quite reach it.

ROD: Well, for Chrissakes, let's get the waitress. Vick—whatsa matter? You come up too soon?

VICKI: I feel a little hot, Rod. Maybe I'd better go freshen up.

ROD: You do that.

(VICKI *exits.*)

ROD: Georgette, I'm a bit concerned with Vicki lately.

GEORGETTE: Yeah?

ROD: Something's fishy. I can't quite put my finger on it, can you?

GEORGETTE: I'm working on it. Maybe I'd better go check on her.

(*Exits.*)

ROD: Great, I'd hate for her to miss the floor show.

NARRATOR: But their romantic powder-room rendezvous is cut short!

(*Gunshot.*)

WAITRESS: Oh, my God! She's been shot!

NARRATOR: As Georgette's perforated remains cool by the powder room, Vicki gives the maître d' the slip.

VICKI (*hands* WAITRESS *a slip*): Could you wrap this for me?

NARRATOR: And is swallowed by the silent orifice . . .

(*Swallowing sounds.*)

NARRATOR: . . . of the night.

NEWSBOY: Extra, Extra! Read all about it! Future carpet queen slays sister-in-law during floor show!

NARRATOR: Vicki, ruthless killer, or just a girl with a lot of luck, all of it bad? We'll find out, after this word from our sponsor!

ROD: That's right . . . House of Shag 'N' Stuff is expanding! We've opened a whole new floor with plenty of eager-beaver salespeople to serve you better! Here's one of them now. Come up here, little lady, and tell us all about it.

SALESLADY: Attention Art Mart Shoppers! We have a blue-light special in the generic modernist department. In order to make room for the new eighty-fours . . .

(*Slashing sound.*)

SALESLADY: . . . Art Mart is slashing prices to the stretcher bars on these late-model masterpieces: Schnabel, Salle, Haring. We've got the brand names you want at prices you won't believe! What's the secret of Art Mart's everyday low, low prices? We buy directly from the artists as they're being thrown out into the streets, and pass the savings to you, the art consumer. And all Art Mart paintings come with our exclusive guarantee: one hundred percent avant-garde or your money back! Remember: Today's kitsch is tomorrow's collectible. Want something that will shock the neighbors for years to come? Let our home-decorating department help you select that very special work-in-progress for any room in the house. And while you're Art Marting, visit the deli and check out the new wiener wonder, Pesto Pup . . .

(*Pup barking.*)

SALESLADY: . . . cuisine on a stick. Thank you for Art Marting!

NARRATOR: But what really happened that fateful night at the salad bar? Was it something in the vinaigrette? Was there someone else who could have pulled the trigger? To many, the flight of the ex-muff diver, future mop squeezer, Vicki, was as good as a confession. What else but terrible guilt could make a woman in heels sprint? For in the cramped quarters of the gay-girl ghetto, blowing your girlfriend to kingdom come could be written off as taking your space! And what about Babs, the hatcheck girl? Their one-night stand left Babs stranded high on the bunny slope of love.

BABS: One night? One night? It was a whole ski weekend at Stoved Finger Lodge.

NARRATOR: Who killed Georgette? And who cares? And what will become of Vicki? Could it be she faces a brighter future in a prison rehab program than in today's saturated word-processing field? And then there's Rod . . . whose entire life soured between the salad bar and the powder room. For answers to these and even more trivial questions, watch for the next episode, "Victim, Victoria."

Stunned by the success of *Shrimp in a Basket*, by which I mean the fact that no one left—the audience had sat through the entire four hours—I left town. I knew I needed some training, that I'd gone as far as I could on intuition alone. So I headed to the Catskills. I got a job slinging matzo brei at one of the big hotels, where I got to watch Shecky Greene, Phyllis Diller, and Lionel Ritchie do their schtick. I also saw Susan Anton do her country-western act, which made me feel a lot better about my lip-synching in the lobster suit. In the daytime I continued digging *The Well*.

Part 2

NARRATOR: The setting: a peaceful New England town. A town like many others, where murder and depravity offer a welcome respite from the tedious convenience of one-stop shopping. Just a town, a town like many others . . . with a gorgeous gendarme who loves girls almost as much as she loves murder. Garnet McClit, lady dick.

GARNET: What I really dig is a girl who's murder.

(*Police station office. Typewriter sounds.*)

NARRATOR: It was another spit-colored Manhattan morning. Al Dente found the usual cornucopia of crimes cluttering his desk at the New York precinct. The police chief was a cop's cop: tough and stringy as a pot roast, with a face to match.

(*Office intercom buzzing.*)

AL: Yeah?

SECRETARY (*through intercom*): Got a make on that DOA, chief.

AL: Okay. Send in Garnet McClit. Looks like this is her baby.

(GARNET *enters.* GARNET *and* AL *stare at each other as the* NARRATOR *speaks:*)

NARRATOR: Enter Garnet McClit, lady dick. An inspired Irish rookie from the concrete backwaters of the Garden State. Being an Irish tomboy left her with two options: the convent or the beat. She went the latter, with no regrets. Once in a while, though, she dreamed of heading someplace more romantic, like Milwaukee, where being a cop and being Irish still meant something.

GARNET: Whatsa scoop, chief?

AL: Your lucky day, McClit. You play it smart, and this'll get you outta parking violations and into the big leagues. You know that new amazon watering hole?

GARNET: The Vixen's Den?

AL: Yeah. Well, the boys just paid it a little visit.

GARNET: Snazzy joint. Food any good?

AL: They couldn't stick around to find out, so they just got something to go. A stiff. Here, read all about it. Didn't take long for those nutty dames to start making pesto of each other. Here, read all about it.

GARNET: Georgette, that's bad.

AL: Big wheel, huh? Well, she's stopped turning.

GARNET: There's going to be trouble, chief. Those Tribads gotta short fuse. When the *New York Pest* gets a hold of this . . .

AL: Forget the *Pest*. When our boys get through rounding up their head honchas, those bra burners won't be able to get together a softball game, let alone a rumble. Gotta line on the suspect?

GARNET: Vicki, yeah. I know her. Who doesn't? Heard she defected a few years back. Word was she'd turned a real Breck girl. Gotta job, boyfriend, the works.

AL: She gave the maître d' the slip. We'll bag her soon enough, though. She can't go too far too fast in those heels. Tell me, how do those Tribads feel towards a girl once she's had a change of heart?

GARNET: I've been sniffing around this scene a long time. I seen a lotta these broads make a beeline for the straight and narrow. But I'm telling you, none of them has made it to the altar yet.

AL: So they take it kinda personal when one of the flock goes AWOL?

GARNET: Let's just say the Tribads are not exactly pro-family.

AL: Are these dames ditzy enough to frame Vicki?

GARNET: No way, chief. Vicki's a lotta things, but she's just not suitable for framing.

AL: Any way you slice it, it's our chance to bust up this daisy chain for keeps.

GARNET: Maybe so. Still these muff divers have been spoiling for a rumble, and now they've got an excuse. There's gonna be one helluva crackdown.

AL: You mean? . . .

GARNET: What I'm saying is this: until you get that word processor on ice, there's not going to be a bisexual between here and Scranton that'll be safe.

(BLACKOUT.)

Lights up in forest scene. VICKI *is running in circles.*

NARRATOR: Vicki ran and ran. Without direction, though not without purpose. But why did she run, if she were, indeed, innocent? Perhaps in her heart of hearts, there was something she longed for more fervently than justice or even her own freedom. A sequel, perhaps? As the Zen masters have said: what is the sound of one hand clapping? Or as the TV moguls restated: what is the use of one great pilot without a thirteen-week run? And so Vicki ran until the wilderness lay all around her. Vicki knew she was lost. Alone with the elements.

DISEMBODIED VOICE OF GOD, OR CARL SAGAN DOING GOD: Oxygen, helium, hydrogen, and whiskey sours—these elements form the building blocks of life as we know it.

(*Twigs snap. Animal sounds.*)

NARRATOR: Or was she alone? Her soul called out to the heavens . . .

(*Phone being dialed.*)

NARRATOR: . . . but as usual got a busy signal.

(*Busy signal. Ominous birdcalls.*)

NARRATOR: Overhead, three bald scavengers circled with the deadly precision of a lazy Susan laden with tainted hors d'oeuvres.

VICKI: Who's there? Yoo-hoo, here I am.

NARRATOR: Somewhere in the uncharted recesses of her mind, Vicki knew she was the heroine and could not be killed off. Not with a series in the offing. Perhaps her old college chum, the writer, might con-

struct a few close calls. She might have to run down a few blind al-
leys, in orthopedically hazardous footgear, bullets of myopic snipers
snagging her nylons.

(*During this narration,* VICKI *acts out her fantasy of
landing a guest spot on a TV detective show. She shifts
into a more operatic mode as:*)

NARRATOR: Or perhaps it would be a gothic affair. She might be com-
pelled to run across the moors, in a flimsy peignoir, nipples baying at
the North Star. But this much was certain: she would be rescued.

(*Footsteps. A shadow approaches and eclipses* VICKI.)

VICKI: Oh, no, no, no, GOD, no. You're not William Shatner.

NARRATOR: William Shatner? Is he in this?
(BLACKOUT.)

Lights up on street scene with GARNET.

NARRATOR: For Garnet McClit, seasoned sapphic flatfoot, Al Dente's
theories were as meaningless as pork fried rice without the duck sauce.
Who pulled the trigger and why? Vicki's guilt was another stale assumption she wouldn't buy and couldn't swallow. Pass the mayo, please.
No, to Garnet, the field was wide open. So that left just . . . everybody. Only problem was—everybody seemed to have an alibi as air-
tight as a Tupperware cake saver. Only person Garnet hadn't checked
out was Babs, the hatcheck girl. Sure, she knew Georgette had a fling
with her. So what? Tribads were known to change partners more times
than masons in a three-legged relay. Would Georgette have jeopar-
dized a promising career in dental hygiene for a few moments of empty
ecstasy with a hatcheck girl? A woman whose phony accent fooled no
one about her bridge-and-tunnel origins. Garnet didn't think so. Still
. . . what about their affair? Just a Sunday drive—or a joy ride through
the Well . . .

(*Scream, sound of falling body, and splash.*)

NARRATOR: . . . of Horniness. . . Georgette was six feet under. Her side of the story died with her. But if she could have talked, what would she say?

GEORGETTE (*voiceover that comes out of nowhere or, more exactly, through an offstage reverb mike*): Just in case you really want to know, Babs was the best-looking thing I ever saw. I got steamed up watching her cross the street. Whatever a broad's supposed to have on the ball, she's got it. My tongue felt a foot thick when we talked, and if she'd asked me to jump, I'd a said, "How high?" So why'd I dump her? I'll tell you this. And you can tuck it away if it means anything to you. I don't like her, and I don't know why.

GARNET: I wished I'd gotten the specs on the hatcheck hussy. I wouldn't know her if she got in bed with me.

(BLACKOUT. OMINOUS ORGAN STAB.)

Lights up in coffeeshop with ROD *and* AL.

ROD: When that deal on the linoleum mine comes through, I'll have the entire home-decorating industry painted into a corner.

AL: Don't get me wrong, Rod, my boy, idealism is great, especially in an election year. But you gotta remember you're talking about South America, you're talking about a lotta Catholics . . .

ROD: What are you driving at, my man?

AL: I'm talking about Catholics, whole different ball game.

ROD: Is it as bad as all that? I mean, they're still human.

AL: Human, yes, but they're afraid of patent leather. They do it in the middle of the day, and eat macaroni and cheese after. They think God is made out of plastic and glows in the dark. Human, I wonder . . .

ROD: I know what you're trying to do, Al, but I gotta dream. Something to keep me going. I'm not going to give it up . . . it's all I got . . . now. I still think we got the right to a few things. To a roof over our head. To a nice piece of shag under your feet.

AL: Don't go too far, my boy. It's not just the Catholic thing here . . . some of these people aren't even white and put that in your pipe and smoke it. Shag, Rod, you're gonna give em shag? These people live in paper sacks and eat what the dog wouldn't touch. And why? Because they're lazy. Too damn lazy to go shopping. And frankly I just don't see how giving away throw rugs to El Salvador is going to change all that.

ROD: Well, it won't. At least, not overnight.

> (*Pinteresque pause. Audience gets nervous, thinking the show has taken a bad turn.*)

AL: Take a tip from me, all that linoleum ain't going to keep you warm at night.

ROD: Whatcha got for me?

AL: I gotta very classy dame for you . . . very low mileage—and she don't take tips . . .

ROD: Can that fish, Al. I'm through with the lousy broads you dig up. The last one was so skinny I coulda sliced semolina on her hipbones.

> (BLACKOUT ON ROD AND AL.)

Lights up on street scene. GARNET.

NARRATOR: Garnet McClit took a long drag on her cigarette and leaned against the tenement doorway. She studied the glowing butt. And flicked it into the gutter. It was eleven-thirty P.M. on the Lower East Side. Most of the natives were just getting up. Then Garnet saw her.

(BABS *enters.*)

NARRATOR: Something strangely erotic about the eyes, the way they seemed to float in her face like two wontons in a hot and sour soup. Her full figure stood out in sharp contrast to the clusters of anorectic club-goers beginning to fill the street. Someone or something in Garnet's brain sent a wake-up call to her crotch. What're you doing at this hour, hon? Pretty girl like you oughta be home, watching the funny-car races.

BABS: It's curtains for me and my gal. Like she just didn't meet my needs. Besides, she was just a runt.

GARNET: You like big girls, huh?

NARRATOR: In the harsh light of the ghetto street lamp, the woman's eyes glittered like a tape measure. Garnet seemed to make the grade.

BABS: That's right. Real big. Like you.

GARNET: Too bad I'm a career girl.

BABS: Oh, I really go for girls with Blue Cross. You don't work around the clock, now, do you, ms. officer?

GARNET: I go home. Alone. To sleep.

BABS: Oh, that's too bad. Guess I gotta go sit on that tar beach all by my lonesome.

GARNET: What tar beach is that?

BABS: Just down the street. Sometimes I get real lonesome up there, just me and my Walkman.

NARRATOR: Watching her turn and walk away made the insides of Garnet's thighs feel like butter left out on a hot stove. But she was too much of a cop to cave in to simple lust. "Just a fleshy little trashpasser, okay, excuse me, that's flashy little trespasser," Garnet thought, as she followed her into the building.

(As GARNET *enters the building,* BABS *clubs her.* BABS *grabs Garnet's gun.*)

BABS: Ooh, picking up a bargain like this puts a girl in a mood for a real shopping spree. Something in the home-improvement line. I gotta feeling a certain carpet salesman might feel like doing some private price slashing.

NARRATOR: Can she be stopped?

(*Organ stab.*)

NARRATOR: Can a clerical worker who's tasted blood ever hope to break in to middle management?

(*Organ stab.*)

NARRATOR: Can anyone be satisfied once they've dipped into the Well . . .

(*Scream.*)

NARRATOR: . . . of Horniness? Even as Babs weaves her wicked web, our hero is engaging in some innocent male bonding in another part of town.

(BLACKOUT.)

Lights up on coffeeshop with ROD *and* AL.

ROD: Hey, buddy, do you see a waitress?

AL: I see this woman in white. But I don't think she's a waitress.

ROD: Why not?

AL: 'Cause she looks like we're sick. What do you think about that?

ROD: I think we are sick, and she's the cure. Hey, nurse, nurse, me and my buddy are dying of hunger.

(WAITRESS *enters. Maxwell House jingle is played.*
WAITRESS *sets cups of coffee down on table.*)

ROD: Miss, is this decaf?

WAITRESS: But you said coffee.

ROD: But I meant Sanka-brand coffee.

WAITRESS: Why didn't you tell me you didn't want real coffee?

ROD: Well, now, miss, Sanka-brand is real coffee; isn't that right, Al?

AL: Sure is, Rod. How about joining us for a cup, miss?

(WAITRESS *exits.*)

AL: You're still thinking about her, aren't ya? (ROD *sighs.*) I'm going to say something, and I don't think you're gonna be able to hear it, but Vicki was a cheap little noodle of a woman. She flunked outta community college and probably killed your sister.

ROD: Lies! Lies! I will not hear it. Vicki went away to school!

AL: Yeah, away to the Hoboken Bilingual Keypunch School. Hardly the Seven Sisters, now is it?

ROD: But I still love her!

AL: Rod, my friend, someday you're gonna find you got off easy; the woman had no depth. Taking the plunge with her woulda been like high diving off the shallow end.

NARRATOR: Rod felt he could forgive Vicki everything, even her fried chicken, if only he could have her back. Suddenly, he felt protective towards her, the way sautéed onions must feel towards calf's liver. Even as Rod finds himself knee-deep in thought, our finely wrought fiction is unraveling in another area.

(*Theme music up under following; probably "America, the Beautiful" would be the most appropriate.*)

NARRATOR: To the north lay the majestic Catatonics; to the work-weary masses these are the promised lands . . . where God's chosen people have chosen to spend forty days and forty nights in the wilderness, on the American Plan. But the granite cleavage did not contain happy memories for Rod. For it was there, during a family vacation, that his other sister, Dinette, had been snatched from their campsite by ravenous raccoons. The family was left stunned and . . . bitter! No more Sierra Club calendars for them! Even with the family in the carpet trade, it was the kind of scandal you couldn't sweep under the rug.

RANGER: They finally found that little tyke. What was left of her, anyway.

DEPUTY: Born with a silver spoon in her mouth.

RANGER: That's probably why they killed her.

NARRATOR: There was no way they could know their daughter lived, nor that the carcass found outside the Winnebago was not Dinette, but, in fact . . . a London broil!

(*Sizzle.*)

NARRATOR: Dinette remembered none of this. Not her brother, Rod, twin Georgette, nor the split-level mediterranean mansion. Suckled by her ring-tailed abductors, she became like them—forced to hunt and prowl by night like the hideous half-human apparitions that haunt late-night TV. Roots, berries, and an occasional Eskimo Pie, on these she thrived. The forest provided her with all she needed, that is—except for one thing she craved the most—entrance to the Well . . .

(*Scream.*)

NARRATOR: . . . of Horniness. But now she had Vicki. She had hit rock bottom! Happy at last! It was a muggy summer night in the mountains. The clouds rested like soggy cotton balls upon the brow of the mountain. It was a night made just for lovers. Somewhere a loon cried.

OFFSTAGE VOICE: Madge, what'd you do with the keys to the Buick?

NARRATOR: From their seclusion in the Christmas tree farm, the wild lovers watched the last rounds of a sudden-death golf tournament. How could they know the danger that surrounded them?

(*Faraway police sirens, drawing nearer.*)

OFFSTAGE VOICE (*yells*): 'Fore!

(*Golf balls start pelting* VICKI.)

NARRATOR: Omigod! She's been hit! And from what I can see, quite badly! Her eyeliner's running down the street!

(*Footsteps.* VICKI *slumps into Dinette's arms.* DINETTE *starts to carry her offstage. We hear footsteps running closer. Flashlight on lovers.*)

RANGER: There she is! Bag that she-devil! Don't let that varmint escape! Somebody call an ambulance!

(DINETTE *drops* VICKI *and exits.*)

NARRATOR: Yes, yes, of course.

(*Dialing sound.*)

NARRATOR: Is there a doctor in the house?

(DOCTOR *enters from audience.*)

DOCTOR: Here I am.

NARRATOR: You're too young to be a doctor!

DOCTOR: I'm a resident. I can do anything a real doctor can do except play mixed doubles. Bring her to my office!

NARRATOR: And so an ambulance bears Vicki away.
                    (BLACKOUT.)

NARRATOR'S VOICE: At the hospital a dedicated team of professionals try to work Vicki in.

Lights up in hospital. DOCTOR *and* VICKI *with nurse, who is* BABS, *acting very bored.*

BABS: No appointment, well dear . . . ah, you're in luck! A cancellation!

DOCTOR: We're here to help you. But you must try to help yourself. Any small detail you can recall is important. Concentrate, how did you get from the nightclub to the mountains?

VICKI: I don't remember.

DOCTOR: What did you do there?

VICKI: I don't remember.

DOCTOR: Who were you with?

VICKI (*hesitates*): I don't know.

DOCTOR: Are you sure?

VICKI: Yes, I'm quite sure. I've just had a terrible shock, you know.

DOCTOR: Yes, kidnapping and loss of memory are terrible, indeed, but nothing compared to the shock you'll get when you pay the bill. Now, dear, I want you to relax and try to forget this nasty amnesia. That's right! Relax and try to breathe normally. Nurse, will you fix a cup of coffee to calm down the patient?

BABS: Certainly, doctor. All right, honey, how do you like it?

VICKI: I don't remember. Oh, doctor, doctor, it's terrible!

DOCTOR: Vicki, what is it?

VICKI: All I can remember is that I left my clothes at the laundry and lost the ticket. Now I don't remember what the bag looked like. Gone, all gone, my favorite socks, everything I ever loved . . . gone!

DOCTOR: Just relax and watch this crystal. You have box seats at a Ping-Pong tournament. Your eyes never leave the ball. You are getting sleepy, sleepy, sleepy . . .

(*Falls asleep and starts snoring.*)

BABS: Doctor, wake up.

DOCTOR: Ah, Vicki, what do you remember?

VICKI: It's no good, my mind's a blank . . .

DOCTOR: Yes, we know that. (*To* BABS:) I'm confident I can restore the patient's true identity.

BABS: You can, but why?

DOCTOR: Prepare twenty-eight cc. of phenobarbothanx.

BABS: Phenobarbothanx . . . *pheno*, as an antibiotic?

DOCTOR: Right.

BABS: And *barbo* . . . as a sedative? And *thanx*?

DOCTOR: And thanx for the memories!

(*Organ stab.*)

NARRATOR: Can the doctor restore Vicki's true identity? Can anyone save Vicki from the vegetable patch? Can . . . wait a minute . . . haven't I seen that nurse before—that's no nurse, that's HER! Omigod! It's the proverbial girl in white-collar clothing. Tune in next week for the startling conclusion of the Well . . .

(*Scream.*)

NARRATOR: . . . of Horniness!

(ORGAN THEME UP. BLACKOUT.)

Part 3
In The Realm of the Senseless

Organ: "The Well Theme."

ANNOUNCER: The Well . . .

(*Scream.*)

ANNOUNCER: . . . of Horniness! Episode three, "In the Realm of the Senseless."

NARRATOR: The setting, a peaceful New England town, just a town like many others, where men are men—

OFFSTAGE VOICE: And so are the women!

NARRATOR: The play that puts lesbians on the map . . . and possibly the menu!

MARGARET DUMONT: Do tell, how are the lesbians today?

BABS: Hot! Mmmmmmmm . . .

GARNET: Steaming . . .

(*Slurping sounds.*)

GEORGETTE: Served in their own juices!

(*Lip smacking.*)

NARRATOR: Tonight's episode.

(*Organ stab.*)

NARRATOR: In our last episode we left Vicki . . .

(VICKI *giggles.*)

NARRATOR: . . . our heroine . . .

BABS: Our heroine? Our heroine! What am I? Chopped liver!

NARRATOR: The plucky pervert who gave up security and a half share in the Hamptons—all because her love for women was greater than her love for self.

(*The following narrative is continuous with overlapping potshots from the peanut gallery.*)

BABS: Maybe they think you died onstage.

NARRATOR: At last, dialogue that reveals the way women . . .

VICKI: Listen, sister . . .

NARRATOR: Really talk to each other.

VICKI: A little piece of advice: you could be put on prerecorded tape.

NARRATOR: This is the play women who love women have been waiting to see!

BABS: Can that chowder! Who wants to see an uptight WASP from the Midwest stumble around in a polyester dress? I'm the one they come to see.

CARMELITA: Who's gonna see you on the radio?

NARRATOR: A collaborative effort—

BABS: This is my big moment! I got my teeth capped for this part!

NARRATOR: Unlike traditional theater . . .

ROD: Hey, hey, girls come on—remember, there are no small parts.

GARNET: There are only small minds, Rod.

BABS: You should know, you've got one of the smallest!

NARRATOR: A proverbial filling up and spilling over of sapphic sentiment!

VICKI: Good things come in small actresses!

BABS: Tell me about it, I came in several small actresses.

NARRATOR: Yes, ladies and genders, our show is another fine example of women working together.

CARMELITA: Where's my lipstick! Which one of you took my lipstick!

NARRATOR: A testimonial to women's love for one another!

BABS: I wouldn't touch anything of yours!

NARRATOR: Of their ability to surmount the limitations of their own egos, to work collectively!

BABS: I'm the star! I'm the star! I'm the star!

NARRATOR: In this, our final episode . . .

ROD: Thank God, I can't take another minute with these dizzy dames.

NARRATOR: . . . we find Vicki . . .

(*Sound of panting, shoes running.*)

NARRATOR: . . . on the lam, in the picturesque Catatonic Mountains. She seems hopelessly lost—

ROD: Well, if it's hopeless, I say let's just put on the laugh track and break out some brews!

NARRATOR: I said *seems* hopelessly lost, Rod.

ROD: Just checking there, buddy.

BABS: She's hopeless, all right.

VICKI: Now just a minute, Babs, you two-bit thespian!

BABS: Who are you calling a thespian? I'm a normal woman! I'm no introvert—like the rest of you.

NARRATOR: Vicki is wandering in a daze.

VICKI: A daze! Oh, don't you think I should wear something that shows off my figure?

BABS: Not unless you're wearing a cast-iron girdle under it!

NARRATOR: We last saw Vicki, prostrate on a La-Z-Boy . . .

(VICKI *snores.*)

NARRATOR: About to get an injection to restore her memory.

BABS: Shall I call you at the hospital, doctor?

DOCTOR: Why? I'll be at the golf course. I thought I could get in nine holes before the *Cosby Show.* (Exits.)

NARRATOR: As the doctor exits, the nurse readies the needle . . . wait a minute—that's no nurse, that's her!

(BABS *hisses, giggles.*)

NARRATOR: Poor Vicki, nobody is there to hold her hand as she gets the prick. What's really in the needle? A regular Florence Nightshade, aren't we, Babs? And how did you penetrate the brotherhood of healing?

BABS: I'm a Kelly girl!

NARRATOR: Babs administers the heinous hypo, only to send Vicki down.

(*Organ stab.*)

NARRATOR: DOWN.

(*Organ stab.*)

NARRATOR: DOWN, into the Well . . .

(*Scream.*)

NARRATOR: . . . of Horniness. Can nothing stop the testy temp worker? She callously climbs over Vicki . . .

(*Sound of* BABS *grunting with physical effort.*)

NARRATOR: . . . who is as limp as a closet case on her wedding night. Babs begins dialing . . .

(*Sound of* BABS *dialing phone.*)

BABS: Hello, I'd like to speak to Police Chief Al Dente . . . no? Well, give him a message . . . tell him he can pick up that touch typist he's been trailing. (*Hisses.*)

(*Sound of phone hanging up.*)

NARRATOR: Meanwhile, down at headquarters, Al Dente was feeling very excited. The Feds had been on the case for weeks. Finally, after combing the area, they had turned up something.

OFFICER: Looks like human hair, chief.

AL: Yes, it does, but that's the beauty of Dynel, my boy.

NARRATOR: Just as he thought, the word processor had wigged out and run. The chief had seen it a million different times before: when the chips were down, the chicks left town. They just couldn't take the heat, and if the heat didn't get them, it was the humidity. The chief was getting pretty steamed up himself.

AL: I'd have the supper-club sniper in the slammer if it wasn't for stupidity.

OFFICER: Sorry, chief, I . . .

AL: My stupidity. I should have never assigned the androgyne to the case.

OFFICER: You mean Garnet.

AL: Sending her out by herself to sniff out a girl was like sending a blind man out without a cane.

OFFICER: I don't get it, chief—

AL: They'd both disappear into the first manhole they'd uncover.

OFFICER: I still don't get it.

AL: That's the last Tribad on the force, you hear me? They've got no ambition.

OFFICER: But Garnet seemed like such an eager beaver.

AL: Even on the ball field—they don't care if they live or die in the bush leagues.

OFFICER: Chief, I got something on my mind.

AL: So spit it out.

OFFICER (*spits*): I can't help but think, well . . .

AL: Well?

OFFICER: Well, maybe you're wrong about Vicki.

AL: Phooey.

OFFICER: I think she's innocent.

AL: If she's innocent, I'll eat her.

OFFICER: But chief, YECH!

AL: You want me to believe the femme was framed? And not only framed but fingered? But by who?

(*Organ stab.*)

NARRATOR: And how many?

(*Organ stab. Sound of phone ringing.*)

AL: Police morgue. You stab it, we slab it. Is this a takeout or a delivery?

CALLER: I gotta little message for Garnet McClit.

NARRATOR: Al Dente cupped the receiver to his ear.

AL: What?

CALLER: Tell her I got her clues. She can pick 'em up anytime.

(*Dial tone and organ stab. "Garnet's Theme" up.*)

NARRATOR: The cryptic call sheds no light on the case at hand. But it did remind the chief that the lady dick had not been spotted since the last commercial. While the chief mused, Garnet was still struggling to regain consciousness. Bab's blow had taken the edge off the sapphic sleuth's ordinarily sharp senses. Even the simplest thing . . . standing up . . . seemed as difficult as putting on a girdle underwater.

(*Gurgle and snap.*)

NARRATOR: Garnet didn't know who or what had hit her. And what of the mysterious woman she had met? "Now she was a knockout," thought the leggy gumshoe as she stumbled home.

(*Sound of key in door.*)

NARRATOR: The detective declined to disrobe but immediately fell into a stupor.

(*Thud.*)

NARRATOR: It wasn't as comfortable as a futon, but it was about all she could afford on her salary.

(*Sound of* GARNET *sitting and lighting a cigarette.*)

NARRATOR: As for the case, it went on the back burner. But in the morning . . .

(*Sound of rooster.*)

NARRATOR: . . . all Garnet's theories were still half-baked. She'd have to scrape something together for the chief.

(*"Garnet's Theme" out. Carpet commercial music up.*)

NARRATOR: While we wait for the punchline, Rod is back at the ranch-style poring over some new carpet commercials.

(*Sound of pouring.*)

ROD: We'll be right back after a word from our sponsor! That's right— Art Mart is expanding! We've opened the first artist colony for has-beens! Deadwood Arms! And here to tell us all about it is my favorite has-been—David Burned-out. (ROD *metamorphoses into David Byrne.*) You may find yourself behind the wheel of a large automobile. And you may find yourself living in a beautiful house, with a beautiful wife.

And you may ask yourself: (*David Byrne becomes a chic Crazy Eddie*)
Holy shit! How in the hell am I gonna pay for this on only five dollars
an hour? Yes! It's true, the good life can be yours even if you haven't
landed a dealer, publisher, or producer. Haven't had a new idea in five,
ten years? You'd be surprised how many artists are saying the same
thing! And if you act right now, you can join thousands of artists
who've found early retirement the answer to their creative crisis!
Deadwood Arms is the perfect place to pack in the palette! Trade in
a life on the cutting edge for a life on the beach! The splendor of
middle-class life is only a phone call away! You can forget about those
bad reviews or no reviews, and all those people who stabbed you in
the back on their way to the top as you relax at our mile-long sushi
bar! And each of our comfy condos comes equipped as a complete
three-room floor-through tenement with tub in kitchen, roaches op-
tional, so all you'll be giving up is the pressure, not the pleasure, of
that wacky East Village lifestyle. Remember, all you blocked artists
out there: it's never too early to GIVE UP!

NARRATOR: But we haven't given up on Rod, though perhaps we should,
for at the moment—

(*Dingdong.*)

BABS: Avon calling!

NARRATOR: But when he opened the door . . .

(*Sound of planes.*)

NARRATOR: This was no saleslady.

ROD: Hey, hey.

NARRATOR: From her careless capri pants to her skimpy halter top, Rod's
eyes swept over her hills and valleys like two pilots on a search-and-
destroy mission, missing only one thing.

(Organ stab and planes out.)

NARRATOR: The redhead was packing a rod!

(Sound of trigger.)

BABS: Okay, Mr. Carpet King, don't try anything funny. Not that that's a danger in this show. I'll make a sister outta you real fast!

(Hospital ambience music.)

NARRATOR: Back at the hospital, a bevy of blondes arrive to frisk our friend Vicki.

BLONDE A: The chief said they're gonna pin this caper on you.

VICKI: What! And leave a mark in my dress? Just let him try . . .

BLONDE B: He said to find something . . .

BLONDE A: Anything . . .

BLONDE B: And make it stick . . .

(Organ.)

NARRATOR: Vicki was almost at the breaking point. She had been pursued all over the state, from hotel to motel. She had lost her curling iron and was—GASP—almost out of Sweet 'n Low. Would this torture never end? Once again she called out to the heavens . . .

(Sound of dialing, ringing. Recording up.)

ROD AS GOD: Hi! Thanks for calling, but I'm not able to come to the phone right now. But leave your name, number, and religious persuasion after the beep, and I'll get back to you.

(Beep.)

NARRATOR: Then she heard the most vicious vixen bark out:

BLONDE A: Spread 'em, sister!

NARRATOR: The command seemed strangely familiar to Vicki. As she complied, she thought . . .

VICKI: PRISON!

NARRATOR: She would have prayed for amnesia, but she didn't know if her insurance would cover a relapse. In desperation, she thought of England. But that was worse than prison!

VICKI: At least in prison they have central heating and decent coffee!

NARRATOR: She felt a hand run the length of her leg.

(*Sound of running.*)

VICKI: Find anything you like?

BLONDE B: Just browsing.

VICKI: Well, if you don't see it, just ask for it. Maybe I have it in the back.

BLONDE A: She's clean.

VICKI: Maybe you should get a second opinion.
                    (HOSPITAL OUT.)

Sound of car doors opening, slamming. Sound of typing.
Police office up.

NARRATOR: Vicki passed up the chair, the sofa bed, and the judge's generous offer of amnesty in exchange for a date, in order to take an all-expenses-paid trip for one . . .

(*Cheers and applause.*)

NARRATOR: UP THE RIVER!
> (GROANS. SOUND OF CELL DOOR CLOSING.)

Jail ambience up.

BABS: No more word processing for you, honey! It's license plates from now on! (*Cackles.*)

NARRATOR: Can Vicki survive her stint in the slammer?

(*Organ keys.*)

NARRATOR: Is it the end of the line for this lezzie?

(*Organ keys.*)

NARRATOR: We'll find out after this word from our sponsor!

(*Disco music up.*)

ROD: It's Saturday night in hip city, and you're a loose woman on the loose—you want to move and groove to the latest beat, you want to go: (*singing*) "Where the boys . . ." aren't!

BABS: That's where *we'll* be!

ROD: If you're like us.

BABS: And we know you are, or you wouldn't be listening.

ROD: You want to cut the rug at your favorite amazon watering hole. And in this town, a town like many others, the place to go for girls is . . . The Vixen's Den! And this month . . . we're having a sale! We've slashed our already low, low prices on wine, women, and song!

GARNET: That's right, the girls are really coming out for this one!

GEORGETTE (*temporarily revived for the purposes of this commercial break*): Why? 'Cause we lost our lease!

ROD: But don't sweat it, theater fans, 'cause, hell no . . .

ALL: WE WON'T GO!

ROD: We're staying put to continue our tradition of quality entertainment for less. These are the same high-gloss performances you'd expect to pay fifteen, twenty, or even fifty dollars for in any other theater or boutique. But at The Vixen's Den . . .

GARNET: Would you believe!

MOE: Four ninety-nine or less gets you live girls onstage without the two-drink minimum. This offer is not available in any store.

CARMELITA: Let me, Carmelita Tropicana, Ms. Loisaida of 1984, be your hostess.

ROD: Only at The Vixen's Den where the laughs are cheap.

GARNET: And the women are free!

ROD: We want you to come and come again! So hurry on down to The Vixen's Den, right off Route seventeen in this town, a town like many others!

BABS: Oh, and tell 'em Babs sent ya.

NARRATOR: Vicki was very upset. She didn't realize the prison uniforms would have HORIZONTAL stripes!

VICKI: Oh, God, I'm all HIPS!

INMATE A: Oh, yoo-hoo.

INMATE B: Howya doing, Goldilocks?

INMATE A (*in a stage whisper*): We haven't had a blonde in a while.

VICKI: Oh, hello, I'm sorry, I'm . . . I've never been behind bars before.

INMATE C: Whatsa matter, don't you drink?

INMATE A: Don't mind her, my little turnover.

INMATE B: Whatcha get sent up for anyway? Mugging an Avon lady?

INMATE C: Scratch somebody's eyes out at the sale table?

INMATE A (*in mock sympathy*): Shoplifting at Bonwit's again, tsk, tsk.

INMATE C: Ah, let up, girls. She's taking it kinda hard.

INMATE B (*lecherously*): That's not all she's gonna be taking kinda hard when we get through with her.

INMATE A: Relax, Goldilocks . . .

INMATE C: We're just trying.

INMATE A: To make you.

INMATE B: Feel.

INMATE A: Welcome. Right, girls?

(*Voices in unison, sound of affirmation.*)

INMATE B: We wish we could make you feel really welcome, but they locked the broom closet.

INMATE A: Shush, you gotta give her something to look forward to . . .

NARRATOR: In desperation, Vicki buries her head in her skirt.

(*Sound of mumbling from* VICKI.)

INMATE C: You might as well get used to it.

INMATE B: Goldiwet.

INMATE C: Honeydung.

INMATE B: Little Miss Pussywet. You're one of us now.

INMATE A: After all . . .

INMATE C: We're *all*.

INMATE A: Sisters.

INMATE B: Under the skin, aren't we, girls?

INMATE C: You could learn to like it . . .

INMATE A: We could teach you . . .

NARRATOR: Vicki began to wail.

INMATE B: Come on, save the wails.

INMATE C: Oh, go on and scream. It'll break the monotony.

VICKI: Let me out! I'm not supposed to be in jail! I'm white, and I can work if I have to!

INMATE B: Oh, leaving so soon? Tsk, tsk, don't let *us* keep you.

VICKI: I don't belong here! This must be a misprint, a typo, I don't like this anymore! And you . . . all of you . . . I don't like you either.

INMATE A: OUCH!

INMATE B: OOH! She really knows how to hurt a girl!

INMATE A: Come to think of it, you may be right.

INMATE C: Maybe you don't like us . . .

INMATE B: But!

INMATE C: You are LIKE us.

INMATE B: Dearie.

INMATE A: And you do belong here with us.

NARRATOR: Vicki knew they were baiting her. But she didn't go for it.

VICKI: No thanks, I ate a heavy lunch.

(*Organ.*)

INMATE A: What happened?

INMATE B: Who turned out the lights?

INMATE C: Damn it all, I told you if you put too many vibrators in one socket, this'll happen every time.

(*Organ. "Garnet's Theme" up.*)

NARRATOR: While Vicki had been incarcerated, Garnet was at home piecing together the evidence until she got a clear picture of the villainess . . . BABS!

(*Hiss. Sound of car.*)

GARNET: I gotta get to the bottom of this.

(*Sound of car speeding up.*)

NARRATOR: Immediately she rushed to the prison, the crime of the scene. Little did our gamy gumshoe know there was no bottom to the Well . . .

(*A splash followed by a scream.*)

NARRATOR: . . . of Horniness!

(*Organ to prison sounds.*)

NARRATOR: During all the confusion, Garnet entered the prison and grabbed Vicki in the dark.

VICKI: That's not the dark.

GARNET: And you're not a real blonde.

VICKI: Bye, girls. Hee-hee.

INMATE B: Don't kid yourself, honey. There's no bi-girls here.

INMATE A: You'll be back too.

INMATE C: Goldilocks.

INMATE B: Sooner than you.

INMATE A: Think.

GARNET: Come on, let's make tracks.

VICKI: But won't that make it easier for them to follow us?

GARNET: Good point. We'll go in my car.

(*Sound of car doors opening and closing—running car.*)

NARRATOR: Vicki instinctively put her trust in Garnet. But she was taken aback by the brunette's casual attitude.

VICKI: Darn, I shoulda asked for a receipt.

NARRATOR: Her fate was in Garnet's hands.

VICKI: That isn't all I've thought of putting in Garnet's hands.

NARRATOR: But for now, Vicki was content. She hated sex in cars.

VICKI: It reminds me of an unhappy affair I had with a geologist that left me between a rock and a hard place.

NARRATOR: Garnet, a dyed-in-the-wool Tribad from the word "come," studied her companion. She was just her type. Garnet, cursed with the kind of carnal appetite that no *single* girl could satisfy, had, in desperation, turned to married women.

GARNET: This Vicki is made of pretty tough stuff.

NARRATOR: All this running around could ruin a girl's hairdo.

GARNET: But not hers, no sir. No listless locks on this lezzie.

NARRATOR: When did that busy, busy gal, our heroine, find the time to tend her tresses?

(*Organ stab.*)

NARRATOR: Finally, Vicki could not stand the silent meeting of the mutual-admiration society.

VICKI: They have me convicted already.

GARNET: You've been holding up fine so far. I know it's been a lengthy exposition, and you're tired. But don't go to pieces on me now.

VICKI: I can't help it. I can't go on much longer like this. You don't know what it's like, always on the go. Living outta a suitcase. If I don't get a chance to go to bed soon, I don't know what will become of me . . . or the show. But YOU probably don't understand. You're not a blonde.

GARNET: No, I'm a brunette, but I have feelings, too.

(*Sound of car swerving.*)

VICKI: What's the matter? Why are we slowing down? Are we out of material?

NARRATOR: Vicki's eyes met Garnet's. Their gazes locked.

(*Click.*)

VICKI: Garnet . . . I . . . I'm a wanted woman in seven states.

GARNET: Make it eight, baby. You're wanted by me in the state I'm in.

NARRATOR: For too long the lady dick had been tortured by the woman sitting next to her . . . but the sight of her breasts jiggling—her thighs were whispering together—was too much. Garnet traced the outline of Vicki's body with her lips. Vicki's passion stirred. Something in her oven of love began to rise.

(*Please feel free to add any sound effect to this section.*
For example, the sound of a spoon scraping a bowl,
doors creaking open. Feel free to go too far; it's the only
way to go in this play.)

NARRATOR: She threw back her head on the car seat. She felt just like a pair of French doors waiting for Loretta Young's entrance.

(*Radio being tuned.*)

NARRATOR: Garnet played Vicki as expertly as a teenager plays a transistor. When she felt she had had some pretty good reception, Garnet moved in on some fine tuning.

(*Radio sounds: "Adam twelve, one Adam twelve.*
Come in, please.")

NARRATOR: A call from the car radio mangles the mood.

GARNET: Roger, I read you.

DISPATCHER: Roger's off tonight. It's Friday.

GARNET: Right. Whatsa scoop?

DISPATCHER: We have a four-eleven under way at the carpet warehouse off Route seventeen.

VICKI: ROD!

NARRATOR: As Garnet and Vicki speed to the scene of the crime . . .

(*Organ.*)

NARRATOR: omigod, that's no radio dispatcher . . .

(*Organ.*)

NARRATOR: That's *her* . . .

(*Organ. Hiss.*)

NARRATOR: You Kelly girls really get around, don't you? And what have you done with Rod?

(ROD *is gagged and mumbling.* BABS *laughs.*)

NARRATOR: Bound and gagged in his own office! And why drag our heroine into this wholesale horror?

(*Organ.*)

BABS: Well, you wanted to see her again, didn't you? Better make it a good look, because it'll be your last. (*Hisses.*)

(*Door creaks open. Echoed footsteps.*)

NARRATOR: Garnet and Vicki enter the warehouse . . .

VICKI: It's kinda quiet in here for a shootout, doncha think?

GARNET: Vicki, a cop doesn't think in a crisis.

BABS: Hold it right there! If it isn't Van Dyke and Van Dick! Well, well, Garnet, we meet again. What took you so long?

GARNET: Search me.

BABS: An excellent suggestion, sucker. We'll start with Ms. Twinkie Tits over here.

GARNET: BABS!

VICKI: Is there something funny about my breasts, honey?

GARNET: Not a thing, dear . . . now see here, this is no way to treat a lady. Where are your manners?

BABS: This is no play of manners, dick, despite rumors to the contrary. This is just business as usual for Tribads.

(*Organ. Mumbling sounds from* ROD.)

VICKI: Rod! Here I am!

(*Dream music starts.*)

BABS: You can't go back to him, sister. If it was him you wanted, you shoulda figured that out a long time ago.

(*Gunshot.* BABS *laughs. Dream music up.*)

ROD: Honey, Vick, it's just a bad dream, wake up. You're with me now, you're safe.

VICKI: I can go back! I will! You'll see . . . I'm gonna be a good wife!

ROD: Wake up—of course, you'll be the best little wifeypoo a man could ever want.

VICKI: ROD! Omigod . . . you're not tied up . . .

ROD: Right you are. I got the night off, so I could take you out to dinner. You musta dozed off while I was on the phone.

VICKI: But . . . I . . . was . . .

ROD: Honey, you were dreaming.

VICKI: But everything seemed so real.

ROD: You know how dreams are. But, darling, I'll tell you what's real . . . you and I . . . why don't you freshen up while I go start the car?

(*Music up.*)

NARRATOR: These are the dreams of the everyday housewife. As carrots in the Cuisinart, so are the sounds in the Well . . .

(*Scream.*)

NARRATOR: . . . of Horniness. Good night and have a nice life.

THE END

Soon after the play was first published, a lesbian director contacted me and said she wanted to do the play, but she thought it would be more interesting if cast with drag queens. I disagreed, explaining that while I loved and felt inspired by drag, I wanted to create roles for women, specifically, lesbians. The notion of women represented by women onstage horrified her; after all, she had a very tony theater education and knew such things were just not done. When I suggested she stage a Charles Ludlam play instead, she replied she was in the market for a text she could deconstruct. I'm still not exactly sure what deconstruction is, but it sounds like something no one in her right mind would want to have done to her work. Whatever it is, fortunately I was able to persuade the director to do it to someone else's play.

The Lady Dick

My mother was addicted to murder mysteries, especially the kind with titles like: *No Blonde Is an Island* and *My Gun Is Quick*. The covers always featured women who managed to be incredibly attractive and totally dead at the same time. After reading a few grocery bags of these books, I began to suspect that murder wasn't the real mystery; these writers just threw in a corpse or two so they could write about what they really wanted to write about, and what they knew their readers wanted to hear about. The real mystery was always women: broads, dames, chicks, molls, princesses, and dykes.

These books were riddled with lesbians; in fact, dykes were one of the basic building blocks of a good murder mystery, along with *beaucoup de* booze, bullets, cigarettes, and, of course, the omniscent dick. I found the representatives of lesbians in these books very attractive. Okay, so they were clearly depraved and usually ended up dead or married—and watching my mother mope around the house made it hard for me to tell the difference—but so did most of the women in most of these books. At least the dykes were sexy, and they always got what they wanted, even if they couldn't hold on to her. I got the impression that bull daggers were lurking around every corner in America, and it was just a matter of time before one of them preyed on me.

When I stared writing *The Lady Dick*, I had a plot in mind, something about a butch lounge singer who strangles women to Burt Bacharach music. Early in the play, I abandoned that ship, although every time I hear the song "This Guy's in Love with You," I start to have trouble breathing. But at some point I started writing what I had read, or what I had read into my mother's paperbacks. I still could make a case for seeing this play as a mystery, but the mystery's not in the plot but in each character, and these are the kind of mysteries that shouldn't be solved but savored.

****

EVA: Good-bye, Garnet. Give my love to you-know-who.

GARNET: I did what she said. I said, "Good-bye." But I gave my love to nobody. The night was young, but the story was old. The air was filled with the sounds of love. (*Enters a bar, The Pit.*)

FEMALE JONES: Bisexual? No wonder you can't hold down a full-time job.

GARNET: It was enough to turn your stomach. The sign outside calls this The Pit. It's no joke. There's another like it outside of Tampa. Same setup. End of the line for those at the end of their rope. A lovely place if you like to swallow your pride and wash it down with under-spiked, overpriced drinks. It's not a dump; it's a dumpster for love's leftovers. Crowded? You bet. That's the problem. Too many snakes in too little grass, so they start eating each other alive. The rest of the world likes to watch. They call it show biz.

(MICKEY PARAMUS *enters.*)

MICKEY: And now, everybody, it's first, runner-up for Mr. Foreplay of 1978, it's Syosett's own Mickey Paramus. Let's give a really big hand to Nassau County's numero uno lady-killer!

(MICKEY *begins to sing, and as she does,*
she approaches each woman at the bar. Her slightest
touch is enough to make the women faint and slide
off their stools. After she has dispatched all the barflies,
MICKEY *addresses the audience while* GARNET *watches*
and comments.)

MICKEY: I hate to admit it, but I'm a great lover.

GARNET: Maybe you should get a second opinion.

MICKEY: It's not my fault. I can't help it. When women sleep with me, they can't keep their hands off me.

GARNET: Kinda the way flies feel about dead meat.

MICKEY: This chick the other night, I gave her ten orgasms.

GARNET: Special occasion, or you just trying to surprise her?

MICKEY: You can't tell me a girl doesn't need that?

GARNET: I don't think I could tell you a thing.

MICKEY: So I'm waiting, right? She's gonna do one of two things. Cry or tell me she loves me. Either way I win.

GARNET: What do you win?

MICKEY: I get to go to sleep, and she gets the wet spot. But this chick, she throws me a real curve. She says, "Whatya got to eat around this dump," and then she steps over me like I'm a dead skunk in the road.

GARNET: Nothing worse than a rude nymphomaniac.

MICKEY: And I say, "Hey! Howsabout some coffee with me before you split? Come on, baby, make me some coffee." And this chick says, "Perk your own poison, daddy-o. I'm having my coffee down the road. No cream, no sugar, and no dumb prick." Good story, huh? Never mind, I already know it's a good story.

GARNET: The trouble with you is that you spend too much on advertising. The good stuff sells itself.

MICKEY: I met some cool chicks in my day, but you're a real Frigidaire. How about if I told you I was dying for you, I hadn't been with anybody for months 'cause I was locked up for five sex crimes, wouldn't you want to come home with me and make it a sixth?

GARNET: Didn't you forget the part about the etchings?

MICKEY: Can't we make a long story short? By tomorrow, you and me could be old friends.

GARNET: Mind if I slip into something more, ah . . .

MICKEY: For me?

GARNET: Only for you.

MICKEY: Will I like it?

GARNET: You're gonna die.

> (MICKEY *freezes*, GARNET *crosses to a pile of shopping
> bags at stage right. She addresses the audience as she
> steps over corpses on the floor.*)

GARNET: For three years I was treading water in the secretarial pool. Now I was about to go down for the third time. Next time, I knew, I'd be doing the dead man's float in suburbia. I got desperate. Any woman would. And what do women do when they go crazy? They go shopping. A new outfit makes for a new woman. (*Strips out of her prom dress and sings "A Butch Is a Woman," by Sharon Jane Smith:*)

A butch is a woman
Who looks like a man,
Depending how close you look.
A femme is a female.
Sometimes she may be male,
Sometimes she don't want to cook.
A femme can be fatal.
A butch can be prenatal,
But everyone knows a dick.
Some walk like their moms,
Some walk like their dads.
It's never too late to switch.

(*Addresses* MICKEY, *who is no longer frozen:*) Okay, songbird, let's see you reach for the stars. (*Points her finger at* MICKEY, *as though it were a gun.*)

MICKEY: Whatsa matter, lady?

GARNET: Don't call me lady; call me ms.

MICKEY: Ms.? What the hell does that mean?

GARNET: It means you're gonna die.

> (GARNET *shoots* MICKEY, *who clutches her groin*
> *and falls to the floor, an agonizing death.* EVA *crosses*
> *from behind the bar and draws a chalk line around*
> *Mickey's body.*)

MICKEY: You gotta draw the line somewhere.

> (*Piano music from an invisible piano.* MICKEY *pulls*
> *herself to her feet as she sings a parody of "Pistol Packing*
> *Mama."* GARNET *remains frozen.*)

MICKEY:

> *Never flirt with a girl*
> *Who's gone down old Lesbos way,*
> *'Cause if you do,*
> *I'm telling you,*
> *Here's what you'll have to say.*
> *Lay that pistol down, babe,*
> *Put that pistol down,*
> *Pistol-packing mama,*
> *Won't you lay that pistol down.*
> *Listen to my story of a green-eyed dick named Clit.*
> *She shot her pistol in the air,*
> *And she hit me in the . . .*

> (MICKEY *grabs her groin and freezes. Blackout.* GARNET
> *begins speaking in the blackout. Saxophone music either*
> *offstage or played by* MICKEY.)

GARNET: It was the usual kind of town. The perfect place to grow up. That's what they said. They also said it was a good place to grow old.

I told myself I'd never find out. I was just passing through.

Where I come from, nothing ever changes. Not the way things are said, not the way things are done. For sure not the style of the clothes because the clothes they wore there had no style. Nobody ever changed their mind. That's why they liked it.

That's right, them and me. Right from the start.

The only good thing about growing up there, the only part I liked, was the weather. We used to have pretty bad weather. Blizzards and tornadoes. On the same day.

You know how it is with girls. One day you're one of them. You're playing with them, and you're all the same. And this makes you happy. Then one day it's different. Because you're different. You know how girls get funny at a certain age. They don't want to do nothing. They want someone to do something to them. Ask their parents for money, so they can dress up like they ain't got no parents. Go around looking like they just got beat up.

I never went through that phase.

When all the other girls started looking for shelter from the storm, I started looking for the storm.

When you grow up different in a town that never changes, it is best to grow up fast and get out of town. No sense being a camel in with the mares.

And I couldn't change. Any more than the town could. Any more than you can change bad weather.

Whatever people were thinking and started saying. Started telling my folks I might be headed down a bad road. But maybe they could head me off at the pass. If I went to a therapist.

So I went to a therapist. And I took one look at that therapist and said, "Okay, bud, drop that legal pad, and stop trying to comb your hair over that bald spot. I know who you are. You're no therapist. You're a shrink. That's what you do, shrink people like me down to size. Your size. Like a lumberjack turning a cow into a pile of jiffy steaks. Well, I got news for you. I'm not your TV dinner. You think you know me. You don't know me. I got better things to do than play word games with someone who wants me to snitch on my own mother. But I'm gonna do you a big favor, head shrinker. I'm gonna let you live. I'm gonna let you crawl on out of here, so you can keep on chargin' people a hundred bucks an hour for an hour that don't even got an hour in it. But you, and your theories, stay outta my way." So you might say I flunked outta therapy.

I know people say therapy isn't the kind of thing you can flunk outta, but that's just something people say.

I did what dropouts do. I left town with somebody else's money. I went to Europe. My parents said they hoped I'd find myself there. That was a nice thing for them to say. Course they didn't really mean it. They hoped I'd find somebody else and become them. Somebody who wore high heels and whistled while she worked.

They didn't have to worry. I didn't find myself. I found her. And I lost what little bit of self I did have.

It was somewhere in the low country. She was seated at a café writing dirty poetry that didn't rhyme. She was a dark and stormy night, and for a while I was her smoking gun.

Then I lost her, too.

By the time I got back to the town that never changes, I had changed. So much, folks didn't recognize me. Cops called me "boy," boys called me "sir," and the ladies . . . well, the ladies just called me.

(FEMALE JONES *enters with a bouquet of flowers.*)

FEMALE JONES: Dingdong! (*Looking at card with flowers:*) Garnet McClit, lady dick?

GARNET (*begins to sing. Music from offstage is heard. The "corpses" come back to life as* GARNET *sings to them the following, sung to the tune of "The Lady Is a Tramp"*):

> *I get too hungry for dinner at eight.*
> *I like the ladies not girls who come late.*
> *I'd never bother to pass for straight,*
> *That's why the lady is a dick.*
> *I'd never go to SoHo in spandex and lace.*
> *I'd never take this show to the American Place,*
> *Rent an apartment and call it a space?*
> *That's why the lady is a dick.*
> *I love to feel three fresh girls in my hair.*
> *Life is a dare.*
> *I'm a dyke,*
> *That's right.*
> *Hetero love, it's old and it's sick,*
> *That's why the lady is a . . .*

(GARNET *is about to kiss* EVA *when* PATTI *approaches
from behind, brings a breakaway bottle down on
Garnet's head. Blackout. Saxophone playing from*
MICKEY, *extreme upstage center. She is barely visible and
backlit.* GARNET *speaks in the darkness:*)

GARNET: The night after I deep-sixed the singer I had a terrible dream.
I dreamt the world was full of housewives without Maytags or blenders. When the world broke down, I found my own way. I woke myself
up but the dream went on.

(*Lights up slowly on The Pit.* GARNET *is alone.*)

GARNET: And that's how I got here. Down by this sewer they call the
river. A little spot just my side of heaven. And I go in and hear this
voice. Like the voice I had been waiting to hear. Like my special angel in my private heaven. Whoever would have thought you'd come
across paradise with the slums breathing down your neck. My angel's
singing for me in gold lamé with fuck-me shoes in a joint with no name.
The guys come here all the time. They don't remember why. But this
is the ticket if you're looking for a little bit of night in the middle of
the day. The joint stinks. Something got trapped in the walls and died.

EVA: Met anybody yet?

GARNET: I'm not looking.

EVA: Don't worry. A girl like you'll meet somebody.

GARNET: I didn't feel like telling her I'd already met somebody. Two
or three times.

ANGEL: Got no appetite? Then why you hanging around the cook?
(*Crosses to bar and perches on bar stool.*)

GARNET: What's a girl got to do to get a beer around here?

> (PATTI *enters with two beer bottles. She places both on table in front of* GARNET.)

GARNET: I said *a* beer.

PATTI: Happy hour.

> (PATTI *crosses to bar, perches on stool near* ANGEL. MICKEY *crosses and approaches* GARNET.)

MICKEY: You come here to hear her sing?

GARNET: Nah.

MICKEY: You know most girls can sing their hearts out, and you don't even notice. Not this angel. Our angel. She takes to the stage the way fire takes to dry wood. A real hot fire. The kind that don't leave no ashes.

> (MICKEY *crosses to the bar and sits down between* PATTI *and* ANGEL. *During the following speech,* MICKEY *flirts with both* PATTI *and* ANGEL. *They are oblivious to* GARNET, *and she, to them. Light from the mirrored ball shines in Garnet's face.*)

GARNET: The way they were talking about her you'd think she could turn this hellhole into paradise by just smiling at you. So I took a look. She was up there. Standing in her personal starlight. Heaven's a heavy ball; you can see yourself in it. The Milky Way starts moving to a Latin beat.
　　　Looking at her, I feel first lost, then found. Like a planet around a star. Her skin's a veil. There's something blue behind it. Her body moves the way a body moves underwater, coming up for air. She's got that something that does something to me. Makes me feel like I'm the person I've always wanted to be. One of the guys.

What an angel she is. Takes away the sins of the world and stuffs them in her bra. It's a living. Wonder if she could keep a secret? I couldn't. Last secret I had left me in Tupelo. That's no place to be without a secret. Wonder if I got real close and hummed a few bars— would she catch on?

Sure I want her. But not just in the worst way. Come to think of it, I don't know what it is I do want. Bet she does. If I died right now, I'd have two requests: clean sheets and her blue eyes.

What about it, Angel? Wanna go somewhere and get good and naked and talk about God? My hands are shaking, and they'll keep shaking till I get my hands on you.

Whatever made me think I was a dick? I'm just another career girl run amok, holding hands with herself on a Saturday night. That's the only way I know how to talk to an angel.

> (MICKEY *grabs* PATTI *and pushes her offstage, then*
> *follows.* ANGEL *crosses to Garnet's table during the*
> *course of this speech.* MICKEY *reappears, in postcoital*
> *disarray and observes the scene. There is the implication*
> *that* ANGEL *is talking about* MICKEY.)

ANGEL: Don't ask. You don't have to ask. You know I'll give it to you. So don't waste your breath. You say you came here to see me.

But it's him you want to hear about. You want to hear about the time when him and me were a thing.

Okay. Don't I always give you what you want?

Sure, I knew Jesus. Wish I didn't. I used to open for him when he was still doing the after-hours places and the freak-show circuit. Now I wouldn't give him the time of day if it were mine to give.

I don't need Jesus no more, you hear! I got my own band. While he's off doing the Las Vegas circuit and the larger country fairs. He used to put on quite a show. With my help.

And that's something you don't hear anything about. You don't hear about the woman behind Jesus, the king of rock and roll, in either the Bible or *Rolling Stone*.

And I'll tell you something else. *We did it.*

And don't act so surprised. What with me out on the road all the time and me gorgeous like I am and him reasonably good-looking, especially in comparison to those Roman guards, some of them bein' three hundred pounds easy and having no dick, well, Mr. Jesus started looking better and better.

Course now this is hushed up, but I was the woman behind the Prince of Peace, and I do mean behind and beneath, though he did have this thing for Peter. Always calling him his rock. Well, Mama did think he was a bit that way, just because he wore dresses.

I said, "Mama, he's a big rock star, that's just the fashion, don't mean nothing."

She said, "Uh-huh."

Well, I don't scare. So I went solo, and he went platinum. I just got tired of the hype. He was good but not that good. I got tired of him inviting all those people over—and I'm talking thousands for some kind of sing-along and supper, and then trying to pretend that two measly fish sticks were going to feed all those people.

I sent out for Chinese, and they paid for me to stay quiet.

Always the image to pump full of hot air. Howsabout the time he drove his Land Rover through the arts and crafts temple, claiming there was no connection between religion and money when I knew damn well that religion had made him filthy rich.

I don't miss Jesus, and I don't miss singing backup to a bunch of lies.

I do know he misses me. You can see it in the act. Gone downhill. He just gets by. How? Reputation. He ain't got nothing to sing about without me. What he does have is a bunch of reheated cover songs and some dick jokes he'd like you to think were an act, but he hasn't had an original idea in I'd say two thousand years.

Thinks he's one of a kind. He's no different than any other honky playing the nigger for the big bucks. Giving heart attacks to fat folks and getting pretty fat himself. Almost too fat to fit into his Jesus suit.

I thought about giving up show biz for religion myself once. That's where the money is. But you know that ninety percent of performing is in the costumes, and I just couldn't, I just could not bear the thought of compressing my considerable talents into one of them blah-colored religious outfits and trying to sing like I'd locked up my pussy and thrown away the key.

It's not natural.

Trouble is with Jesus, he started thinking he was too good for a bunch of beer drinkers. Started thinking he was doing something more than just entertaining. Not your Angel.

Don't worry if everything I said was the truth or not. Haven't you had enough truth for one lifetime? Trust me, I even do my own hair. And you can't ask for much more from a star.

And don't think of me as a fallen angel. Because I didn't fall; I jumped. (*Approaches* GARNET.) Looks like you could use a bit of salt air.

GARNET: If I do, I'll take my margarita over by the air conditioner.

ANGEL: You and me could cover a lotta ground in a hurry.

GARNET: I like it here.

ANGEL: You won't like it when I'm gone. This is a dirty place. And I cover up a lotta the dirt. And I'm going. You're gonna be wishing you were at my place.

GARNET: I'm not the kind to impose.

ANGEL: Not even if I asked you nicely?

GARNET: Maybe.

ANGEL: I'd like to try it. It'll be a new experience. I never had to ask for it before. You'll like my place. It's snug. Can't even turn around. But you won't want to. The air is always warm and wet. Good for your skin. I almost forgot. The ocean's there too. You might want to take a peek. In the middle of the night you can see forever.

GARNET: What's so great about forever? I like the way things are right now.

ANGEL: You make that up right now or steal it from *Reader's Digest?*

GARNET: You don't need the ocean. A girl like you could drown in a whiskey sour.

> (ANGEL *and* GARNET *begin an elaborate cat-and-mouse game with the big band music coming from an offstage jukebox. By the time the song has ended,* GARNET *and* ANGEL *are in an embrace. Suddenly, and without apparent provocation,* ANGEL *pushes* GARNET *away.*)

GARNET: I'll . . .

ANGEL: Don't bother.

> (ANGEL *exits.* GARNET *crosses to the bar.*)

EVA (*begins to sing "Misled," by Sharon Jane Smith*):

> *You got good teeth,*
> *Great smile,*
> *But, honey, you know you're misled.*

GARNET: She left me with nothing but a good long look at her legs. The best souvenirs I've had. It's all in the stockings. Pretty old-fashioned for a girl with such modern ideas.

EVA:

> *You've got great legs,*
> *Great legs,*
> *But, honey, you know you're misled.*

GARNET: Those seams. I kept thinking those seams were like a couple of back roads up through the highlands to a secluded spot. Been there once, think you've died and gone to heaven.

EVA:

> *I ask you a question,*
> *But you don't answer me straight.*
> *Tell me what you do know,*
> *You little so-and-so.*

> (*It appears as though* EVA *and* GARNET *are going to kiss*
> *when* ANGEL *enters, taking stage like the true diva she*
> *is and spoiling, perhaps forever, Eva and Garnet's*
> *moment.*)

ANGEL: I'm here, and that's what matters. Before don't matter to me. And if I don't care about my past, why should you? If I told you where I come from, it wouldn't mean nothing to you. Wouldn't mean nothing to nobody. The name of that town's a dirty joke in a dead tongue.

When Mama was big enough to cross the street by herself, she had me. She didn't look like the kid she was with her white hair and no eyelashes. They tell me that's what comes from standing too close to the fire.

The fire's got nothing to do with Daddy. Most times he's sacked out on the La-Z-Boy like a boiled chicken on a bed of white rice. The rest of the times he's down there. Mama says he's foolin' with cherries. And I say: "Mama, he should wait to pick them. No juice in them little cherries."

"But that's how your Daddy like his fruit. Small and young and hard." Mama knows.

I know them little cherries are just for looks. No good for eating. They go bad before they get ripe.

So I got to see for myself. And I seen him in there, picking. Picking and doing the nasty thing. He was down there with those pink and yellow girls, and them cherries were falling on their heads like little red bullets, but that didn't stop them from doing the nasty thing.

Daddy caught me and sent me to my room, saying that I'd never get a hot meal again.

Mama?

She didn't say much. Just that when I'm older I'd understand. One thing Mama did understand is that there'd be no happy ending to her story. Just clean sheets and boredom in a nice neighborhood. She was still up at midnight boiling everything she could get her hands on. Sitting in the light of a dry moon, my mama was crying all night into her mashed potatoes.

I started getting a lot older that night.

You might as well do it, or it'll get done to you. The boy next door dropped his pants and showed me his thing. Proud, like it was something you could win. It was no trophy, believe me. More like the booby prize.

He said to me, "Didn't nobody ever tell you it's only meat?"

And I knew right then I was a born vegetarian, a real picky eater. I wasn't like a lot of other girls who'd put anything in their mouths and never ask where it'd been before. They don't care much for girls who like to cook for themselves in this dirty-joke town. They got nothing to do but earn a living, and that's just being a slave so you can sleep and eat.

I told my tale to the girl down at the pump. She's a fix-it girl and mighty good with her hands in general, so I thought she might be able to fix me up but good. She offered to fill me up for nothing.

Then she said, "Slide over, sweetheart. You and me and this tin chariot are making a run for it. When we get outta town, I'm gonna buy you a red dress and take you out for a real chicken dinner."

I musta passed out from the excitement.

When I came to, we were already in Saint Louis. But they were out of chicken. The chickens were laying but not hatching. Seems like the hens had all flown the coop. The waiter tried to slip us a breaded veal cutlet when we weren't looking, but I can't look at beef when I gotta taste for girls.

The fix-it girl said she'd make it up to me. Give me a tour of Missouri. Well, I was in quite a state. The show-me state. But she drove me to the zoo.

And I said, "Hold it right there! You think I came all this way to see a show of wild pussy. And I'll do better than that. This pussy's not in chains."

It was her turn to pass out.

When she came to, we were already in the motel. But she didn't know what to say. Then I'll say it. Three little words: "Do it, baby, do it."

(ANGEL *exits. Blackout. Mickey's voice is heard.*)

MICKEY: Oh, yes, ladies and gentlemen—the moment you've all been waiting for. That's right, it's Miss Patti Melt Smith, who's been break-ing records and shattering the sound barrier wherever she's allowed to perform. Let's give her a warm hand . . .

ANGEL (*in a stage whisper to* EVA): And a cold shoulder!

(*Lights up.* EVA *and* ANGEL *at the bar.*
PATTI *strikes a showgirl pose.*)

PATTI: Ta-da! (*Pause.*) Okay, don't clap, leave. You think I need an audience to put on a show? I'm not just an entertainer. I'm an artist! You know what? I'm glad you don't like me. If you liked me, I couldn't like myself. You wouldn't know art if it got in bed with you. Go on home and watch TV, your life's a rerun anyway. You want to be somebody's audience, go ahead. Go watch Johnny Carson. Drool on Joan Collins. You think Johnny's ever gonna laugh at any of your jokes or try to sell your book? You think Joan'll ever drop her dress for you and let you kiss her tummy-tuck scars? And when you die, you know what'll flash before your eyes? Not your life, because you don't have a life. Your life's a dumping ground for other people's garbage. You spent your life watching other people have a life, and in the last moment of your secondhand existence, my songs are going to flash by. They're going to make sense to you on your deathbed. You'll hear them as you exit from the bar and grill of earthly existence.

(GARNET *enters. She stands upstage of* PATTI, *who is unaware of her presence.*)

PATTI: You'll be my captive audience. You're gonna wanna clap, but it'll be too late. I'll be singing, but you'll be dying. You're gonna die loving me!

(PATTI *starts to exit, as she crosses, runs into* GARNET.)

PATTI: Oh, sorry. I just like to warm up a bit before shows. Wait a minute. What are you doing around here? You're a dick. (*Pause.*) That's what you are—a dick!

GARNET: It's a job. I don't like it. I just do it.

PATTI: Don't go telling me about dicks. I've been around long enough to know who's a dick and who's not, and what it is a dick does. Poke and prod and stick himself where he's not wanted, that's what.

GARNET: That's not what she does.

PATTI: She? I don't get it.

(GARNET *is wearing a fedora. Her hair is tucked up*
under the hat. She removes the hat, shakes out her hair.)

PATTI: A she-dick! But it can't be!

PATTI and GARNET: But it is.

PATTI: Why a dick?

GARNET: I don't ask, and you don't want to know. It's like love.

PATTI: How's it like love?

GARNET: When you fall in love, do you ask whether you slipped or got pushed?

PATTI: I still don't get how you can be a dick and a lady at the same time.

GARNET: Don't you ever go out late at night?

PATTI: Sure . . .

GARNET: Alone . . . (*Begins to cross the stage to exit.*)

PATTI: Sure. Hey, wait a minute, what are you trying to sell me?

(GARNET *exits. Abrupt change in lighting. Lights up full,*
bright white suggesting a cafeterialike ambience.)

MICKEY: And now a word from our sponsor. How do you handle a hungry man? The Manhandlers! We've been traveling all across America, asking women how they handled the hungry men in their lives. And now we're in the Poison Oak View Mall in lovely Tupperware Heights, Ohio, with Miss . . .

PATTI: Patti Melt.

MICKEY: Miss Patti Melt! I like to think of America as a big country full of big appetites, and whether he's riding herd on the secretarial pool or blowing up buildings in midtown Manhattan or just keeping the front stoop warm, there's no end to the way guys can work up a man-size appetite. And when that special guy brings that special craving home to you, Miss Patti Melt, how do you handle a hungry man?

(FEMALE *and* ANGEL *enter from opposite sides of the stage. They wear a few articles of male attire over their regular costumes.*)

FEMALE and ANGEL: Dingdong!

FEMALE: Hey, you look good enough to eat.

ANGEL: Stuffing? I'm staying!

PATTI: Gosh, I never saw these guys before.

MICKEY: Do you dread unexpected dinner guests? Ladies, don't let company catch you with your pants down. It's a cook-or-be-eaten world, and a single girl's got to keep a Manhandler around the house.

PATTI: I've never missed with this number. (*Holds up her fingers as if they were guns.*) And I've got dessert too.

MICKEY: Gee, if that don't take the edge off a guy's appetite, I don't know what will. But you oughta save those special recipes for a special occasion—like your wedding night! I can tell there's no meat in your cupboard, but now you gotta handle a couple of wild and crazy carnivores.

FEMALE: How about I pop a little pepperoni into that toaster oven? (*Begins to blow up a long balloon in as menacing a fashion as possible.*)

ANGEL: I got a hot dog and some steamy buns for you! (*Making obscene gestures with a balloon in the direction of* PATTI.)

PATTI: That's no wiener. That's not even Spam. It looks like a penis, only smaller.

(*Angel and Female's balloons deflate as noisily and vulgarly as possible. They exit.*)

MICKEY: That's quite a Manhandler. Miss Patti Melt. Tupperware Heights, Ohio. Of course, it's only a serving suggestion. Personally, I prefer my men lightly breaded and deep fried! Send us your recipes, America, to the Manhandler, care of this station.

(MICKEY *exits.* PATTI *continues to wave to the audience as if the rest of her life were to be an endless endorsement. Lights come down to precommercial level.* GARNET *crosses to* PATTI.)

GARNET: Aren't you going to give Rita Mae Brown credit for that line?

PATTI: She mighta said it, but I lived it!

GARNET: And you may ask why I'm a dick. Maybe there'll be day, and maybe we'll live to see it, when something other than a bulge in the pants will get respect in the streets. Until then, I'm not taking any chances.

PATTI: Doesn't it still get hard for you? Don't they think? . . .

GARNET: They think what you thought . . . That I'm a guy.

(FEMALE *sticks her head through the upstage*
right exit.)

FEMALE: Hey, are you a guy or what?

GARNET: Why don't you suck my dick and find out?

(FEMALE *disappears.*)

PATTI: There's still a few things I gotta know first. Did you ever meet a cop you liked? Did you ever run across a case you couldn't crack? Did you ever meet a girl who said no?

GARNET: I never gave her the chance. When I see something I want, I take it.

(*Pause.* GARNET *takes her time but finally*
kisses PATTI.)

GARNET: Wanna go somewhere and lie down?

(*They exit.* LETHAL WEAPON *enters, either from the*
audience or from the entrance to the theater. If she uses
an outside door, it should be locked behind her. The
audience and the performers should all feel as though
they were being taken hostage.)

LETHAL WEAPON: I know what they call you. They call you sucker. And I know what they call this place. They call it a rathole. Oh, it's not my name for it. I like to think of it as a rattrap, because the rats that are here can't get out, isn't that right? I think there's a couple of rats backstage—why don't you come on out? I feel like buying you a drink.

(*Enter two women,* VICTIM ONE *and* VICTIM TWO. *They*
cross to bar area, behaving as hostages. Whether or not
they are innocent bystanders is open; they
believe they are.)

LETHAL WEAPON: Now you know I know what they call you. But you don't know what they call me. They call me Lethal Weapon. There's been so many, I only remember the first ones, that look on their face the second before they . . . (*hands* VICTIM ONE *a cocktail glass*) drink up, honey. It's not my fault. It's yours.

Before I met you, I could do two things at the same time. Now I can only do one thing to one person. You. You made me a real Johnny One Note.

Lucky for you it happens to be a helluva note.

Before I met you, you were already sleeping inside me like a little germ waiting to turn into a big disease. I was a real nice person. Hard to believe? It was loving you that brought out the killer in me.

I was going to get married. I had a real nice guy, money in the bank, didn't want a thing, and if I did, it wasn't you. My fiancé was a sensitive man. He was going to give up meat after we married. I'd look into his eyes and see baby booties. He loved me so much it made me sick. He used to grill me steaks on the patio. His baby blues'd get all watery, and I'd wonder: is it love . . . or steak sauce?

After all this time, I still don't know. But I guess you know what I did. I ran out onto the patio and I grabbed his flaming sirloins and I hurled them as hard as I could and I set his lilies on fire. Then I turned on him. He was a good man but loving me had made him worthless. He was the first.

Then I went to see my mistress. She wears a beret and talks with this cute little English accent she picked up at a yard sale. We talk about ART. She goes for that funny music. You know the kind I mean. The singers sound like two epileptics screaming at each other in a foreign language. Then there's the instruments. And I am not talking about your piano or your guitar. I am talking about your steamroller and a dump truck running into each other.

I like it. You just can't tap your toe to it.

But she finds the music inspirational. Says it makes her want to do funny things, like make *art*. She makes art to the music. She takes Fiesta Ware . . . my Fiesta Ware, and smashes it to the beat. Then she takes photographs of the damage. The photograph is the art part, the rest is just process, isn't that right?

Myself, I hate art. I miss my Fiesta Ware. I tell her, "I really loved that lavender turkey platter you demolished for your Guggenheim grant."

And she says, "If you love something, SMASH IT. That's the meaning of modern art. And I'm going to make an artist out of you if it kills me."

Well, that was a funny thing to say to somebody who had a killer sleeping inside them. Though I can't say she lived to regret it.

Then I met you. I didn't know, but you might be some kind of cat fancier. So I walked right up to you and said, "Did you see my pussy? It'll come if you call it."

Well, you looked to me as if you were a little bitty frightened Peter Cottontail and I was a great big runaway Chevrolet. Then I got it. You liked being hunted. I could tell the way you let me get close enough to you to catch your scent. Then you went bye-bye.

And my heart started beating like a hammer against a teacup. I caught up with you, yes, I did, in a mall bookstore. You bought me a little present, then you threw it at me.

You said, "I love Georgia O'Keeffe, she's my favorite painter." And I said, "I am Georgia O'Keeffe."

Course, you already knew this. That's why you loved me so much. Over the discount cookbooks, we kissed. You left town.

You left me in a bad way, baby. I wanted you so much I could barely walk. Every time I sat down, I ruined the chair. I didn't dare cross my legs.

Then the phone rang. I hoped it was you. I knew it was you— I had killed off everybody else by then.

It was you. You said, "A storm's coming, and I got to see you." I don't say nothing.

And you say, "Forget about art, give up marriage, I want you." Still I don't say nothing.

And you say, "What's the matter, baby, can't you come?"

And I say, "When I come, you're gonna know about it. But you watch out. I got no brakes."

You said, "Don't stop for nothing."

So I didn't. I got into my car, and I'm driving. And it's raining, then it's hailing, then it's thundering, and then it's lightning and then . . . all of a sudden the STORM STARTS.

There is a wall of water on one side and a wall of fire on the other, and the road behind me is history. There is a trailer park over my head. An entire department store with blue-haired salesladies still trying to hang on to the sales tables, spinning around like in spin the bottle, where it'll stop nobody knows.

It occurs to me this could be the end of life as we know it. I think you and me are going to have a good time.

I get to your house. You take me in. You say something so sweet. I still remember it. Why don't you say it again. SAY IT.

VICTIM ONE: Isn't there something you want to say, like I love you?

LETHAL WEAPON: Shit no. I don't love you. I LOVE YOU. You get it? You got it. Still you insisted on telling me these stories that weren't exactly funny, but I laughed anyway, so hard I slapped your thigh, and you nailed my hand down.

We kissed, and the rain let up. We kissed a little more, and the fog started coming in. I thought if I'm gonna get out, now's the time. Looks like a three-day blow is heading our way. In a few days, I'll be socked in.

I should have got suspicious when you asked me to wear your dead mother's negligee while you got dressed up in your dead brother's Eagle Scout uniform. The moment of truth came in your parents' bed. Before I could ask for more, you were bye-bye.

(VICTIM ONE *exits*. LETHAL WEAPON *turns her attention to* VICTIM TWO.)

LETHAL WEAPON: Of course, I went after you. I had no gas, I had no brakes, and the storm was having a relapse; but I was doing eighty-five in no time.

I didn't even feel the little old lady. The first little old lady. Besides she had eight incurable diseases and no pets, so I figured her time was up. I felt a little bit bad about the family of five.

The first family of five.

Then I remembered my constitutional right to the pursuit of happiness, which says: even if there is no such thing as happiness, I got a right to pursue it.

That's the way it is with me now. Hit and run. I'm gonna run down everything that gets between me and you. Sometimes I feel bad for the people I kill; there's nothing wrong with them, except that they're not you, and that's reason enough for them to die. I know it's just a matter of time before you and me get back together and cause another little earthquake or something even worse.

Until then, I send roses to the kin of my victims. We are talking massacre, and I can't stop till I get to you.

(*Blackout.* GARNET *and* EVA *are seated at the bar.* CON
CARNE *enters but is not seen by* EVA *and* GARNET. ANGEL
and PATTI *enter.*)

ANGEL (*looking at* GARNET, *to* PATTI): She's a bitch.

(ANGEL *and* PATTI *see* CON CARNE *at the same time.*
They are totally intimidated by her.)

CON CARNE: Welcome to my bar, Garnet.

GARNET: Con Carne!

CON CARNE: I see you no like my little present I give you.

EVA: Con Carne gave you something?

GARNET: A one-way ticket to nowhere. You shouldn't have.

CON CARNE: You would have preferred that I pierced your ears with a forty-five? I think that no. But when Con Carne gives, she expects gratitude. Con Carne is hurt.

GARNET: You'll get over it. In the meantime, shouldn't you be checking on those rent-a-goons you got parked out front, the ones with the machine guns in their laps. What are they supposed to do, enforce the two-drink minimum?

CON CARNE: Con Carne does not take insults from girls like you!

GARNET: Aren't you and I the same kind of girl?

CON CARNE: Once, *sí*. Now Con Carne is a new girl. She learns to play with the boys. She go, how you say it, straight to the top; first she go straight, and then she go to the top.
    That is how she get her new name, Con Carne. It means "the hot stuff with the meat." And still Con Carne does not forget the girls she left behind. Girls like you. She gives girls like you a place to play, a place like this, where women can do terrible things to each other. What's the matter, Miss Dick, you no like to play, you afraid to lose?

GARNET: I never lose. It's the rules of the game I hate.

CON CARNE: Maybe your luck is gonna change, what you think?

GARNET: I think you never got over being a B-grade canary in that banana republic. I think you wish you could make it up to B-grade here, but in this neck of the woods, you're pretty strictly bottom of the barrel.

CON CARNE: You do not talk about my island this way. You know nada about my island.

Once my island was just a little country in the big land. But one day we cut the ropes that tie us to this country, and we float out to sea. We are in the middle of the sea, all alone, and we drop anchor.

We are happy to be an island. The gods, they smile upon us. They send us barbecue ribs and potato salad to tell us we are blessed. We no kill, we no work, we don't even have to order out! The rivers they run with rum. In the trees, the fruit. In the bushes, the girls. Everybody gay!

Then one day your people come. Now they no work. Now we work for them. The gods no longer send us Chinese food no more. We are no longer the children of the gods. We have to work for what was once free. By our sweat do we earn our piña colada!

Pero me gente es fuerte. My people are strong. The men, they turn into snakes. They wear shiny pants and drive sportscars. White on the outside, red on the inside. They frighten the young, pale women.

Your people decide the ocean we live in is too valuable for my people. In the middle of the night, they tow our island to a cheaper ocean.

On that night, I, Con Carne, kill six men from the Cleveland of Ohio, and I laugh as they die. Then I jump into the ocean. Con Carne has blood on her hands but a song in her heart. Con Carne swim and swim. All day with the fishes. She become smart like fish. You hear this before, the seafood is brainfood. *Es verdad.*

By the time Con Carne get to shore her head is so tired from being so smart. Con Carne get rich quick. She take money like fish take worm, smart fish. She no take the hook, so Con Carne, she rich and free. Con Carne is not poor, no! Whatever Con Carne wants she buys. No better! She charges! Con Carne have much *dinero de plástico.* She get everything, even the sex! You hear this before—"bisexual"? Is American way, no? (*To* GARNET:) You are the *primera* that Con Carne cannot buy. You try to make Con Carne feel poor. If I am poor, you are tough. You are a real, how you say it, dagger of a bull! *Sí*, very tough, as long as you have a beer in one hand and a blonde in the other. Who gives you these lovely things? Con Carne! *Claro*.

But on the streets is different story, I think. You got no job, no place to live, you don't even know how to put on the lipstick.

De repente—suddenly, you are not so tough. Outside Con Carne's bar and grill you are a dirty joke. They see you and they think you are a runaway from freak show. When there is nothing *buena* on the TV, you are what they watch for laughs.

So, go on, lady dick, where you gonna go to meet the girl? The *supermercado*? Where you gonna go to be tough, Bloomingdale's?

You look pale, *mi amigita*. I think this place is not so good for your health. And your health is all you got now. You spend too much time asking the wrong questions of the wrong people. Too much time in my bar, talking to my customers.

You should take up running. *Sí*, the running for you. Starting now, to run for your life.

>   (CON CARNE *points her finger at* GARNET *as though it were a gun.* GARNET *grabs her, dips her arm across her lap, and kisses her. A long kiss.* CON CARNE *trembles all over, then goes limp and slumps to the floor.* MICKEY *steps over comatose* CON CARNE *to address the audience.*)

MICKEY: Early in the morning Poppa would get me up to go fishing. Nothing to say. Too early in the morning for words. Just bait the hook and wait. Somewhere down, there's a real beauty, a keeper, circling your hook. Wait and wait. Then there's that pull. You feel her.

Poppa'd say, "She's flirting with you. Stay still. Let her tell you when. She's just nibbling. Let her swallow the hook all the way down, give her a chance—then you got her."

One day Poppa don't wake me up to go fishing. Later in the day he's looking funny at me, like he don't know me. Didn't know what to do with me. Too big to sit on his lap, too little to give away. He picks me up and carries me down to the water. But he don't put me in the boat. He puts me on a big sawhorse, slaps the slats and yells, "Giddy-up."

Then he gets into the boat and disappears. For a long time I sat there, pretending to go somewhere. Then the snakes come out of the woods. Never seen so many snakes, and they're coming right for me. I keep thinking they're good snakes. But there's so many I start thinking maybe these aren't the good snakes. I don't know if they can climb or not, but I'm not waiting to find out, so I start screaming.

Nobody comes but more snakes. I'm screaming till I lose my voice. Lucky for me I get a new voice, and those snakes roll over like beagles and start sawing logs. Musta been the good snakes after all.

Must be I'm a snake charmer. Guess every girl's a snake charmer sometime or other. She doesn't know she can do it till she has to.

GARNET: That's about it. There's a lot of people planning to clean up this town. But I'm making sure there'll always be a wrong side of town. My side of town. I think you got my number. If you don't, don't worry. If you're in trouble, or just looking for it, you'll look me up. If you need me, you'll know where to find me. I'd like to show you a little trick. (*Pulls out a deck of cards.*) Anybody got a dollar?

> (*Plant in the audience hands her a five. Pause.* GARNET
> *plays with it, folds it, and sticks it in her bra.*)

GARNET: Thanks. Good night.

(BLACKOUT.)

THE END

Dress Suits
to Hire

F ollowing the success of *The Lady Dick*—again, with success
defined as it was earlier, not in terms of reviews or money, neither of which the show got, but by the fact that most of the
people who came to see the show stayed for the whole thing—Lois
Weaver and Peggy Shaw asked me to write a play for them. I was thrilled.
Lois and Peggy represented two-thirds of the Obie-winning theater
troupe Split Britches, which made them the Lunts of lesbian theater.

My girlfriend has remarked that this play seems more ambi-
tious than the two earlier pieces and wondered if I was feeling more
confident when I wrote it. I'm sure I'll never feel as confident as I did
when I wrote *The Well of Horniness*, because I had absolutely no idea
of what I was doing and what kind of trouble I was getting myself into.
Actually there were a few other theatrical projects—I can't quite bring
myself to call them plays—that preceded *Dress Suits to Hire*. I still enjoy
the titles: *My Life as a* Glamour *Don't*, *Two Guys Who Are Girls*, *I
Married a Lesbian!* and *My Prince Has Come*, but the scripts were strictly
stream-of-cappuccino and hardly worth the cocktail napkins on which
they were written. Still, I think these productions were critical in my
artistic development in that they allowed me to get the following out
of my system: lip-synching while wearing giant animal costumes, break
dancing for the elderly, and a meditation on low-tech printmaking and
Christian iconography that I called *The Potato of Turin*.

Still, writing the play presented challenges I hadn't experienced before. First of all, the fact that Lois and Peggy had been lovers
for years removed my primary motivation for writing: getting girls. It
was hard for me to imagine why someone would go to all the work to

write a play if there was absolutely no chance she would get laid as a result. What was the point?

Fortunately, I had a good job at the time. By "good" I don't mean it was either secure or high paying. It was a temp job in the school-book division of a big publishing house, but it was a good job in comparison to the other jobs I'd had in New York, which included: hot-gluing albino ermine tails to leather scarves, dusting dying plants in the Grand Hyatt Hotel, working for an art dealer who had stolen a Matisse painting, stretching canvas for an artist who paid me in bottles of scotch, and more waitress jobs than I care to remember.

I worked in the inventory department, and part of my job was sending out orders to destroy books no one wanted to buy anymore. One of the books I was asked to destroy was called *Guidelines for Racism and Sexism*. I'd start taking apart the title word by word, wondering just what the guidelines were and who was setting them and why no one was interested in them anymore, and pretty soon I was in that alpha-state so conducive for writing. Because destroying books went against everything I believed in, it filled me with a perverse sense of power, which soon replaced sexual obsession as my creative fuel. The other good aspect of this job was a boss who looked the other way when I took time I could have been burning books to write sapphic smut.

But basically I went about writing this play much as I had *The Potato of Turin*. I took all my obsessions and threw them into the Cuisinart, then I went looking for props and costumes. Pier One Imports was having a great sale; I managed to get a bunch of light-up plastic tulips, a six-foot-high yellow fan, a hula hoop, a couple of slightly used magic tricks, and an I Love NYC piggy bank. This is what theater people mean when they talk about workshopping a play; you have to do your shopping before you can get to work.

A note about the names: I was homesick for my homestate, so I decided to make her a character in the play. She has two emotions: ice and mud. Deeluxe is named after a cow I once loved, a long, long time ago.

****

DEELUXE and MICHIGAN *are seated as the lights come up.*
Deeluxe's chair faces upstage; Michigan's, downstage.
They are facing each other as DEELUXE *begins to sing*
"Run, Run, Run," written by Peggy Shaw. Gradually,
Deeluxe's attention focuses on dressing herself, specifi-
cally, on putting on nylon stockings as she sings.
MICHIGAN *faces upstage, mouthing the words silently.*

DEELUXE:

Gonna fill my mouth with red wine,
Gonna fill my head with cement,
Gonna fill my ears with cotton wool,
Gonna fill my nose with cocaine,
Gonna buy myself a diamond ring,
Gonna get me on a fast train,
Gonna pack my soul in a handkerchief,
But will you be there when I come back again?

I will go where you will never find me,
I will change so you won't recognize me.
Everything I know I'll leave behind me,
A distant memory of all the things there used to be
When there was only you and me.

I'm gonna run run run,
Catch me if you can.
I'm gonna run run run,
Catch me if you can.
I'm gonna run run run so far away,
But will you be there when I come back again?

You're gonna sit down in your easy chair,
You're gonna look out of your window,

You're gonna fill your lungs with nicotine,
You're gonna bite your nails down to the bone,
You're gonna buy yourself a diamond ring,
You're gonna get you on a fast train,
You're gonna pack your soul in a handkerchief,
But will I be there when you come back again? . . .

(*Deeluxe's right hand starts to choke her own neck until*
she falls to the floor, apparently lifeless. In fact, she is
dead for the rest of the play. It seems rigor mortis has set
in rather early. MICHIGAN *is facing upstage. In her lap a*
*small white dog of a mechanical species—*LINDA*—begins*
barking. MICHIGAN *turns around to see what* LINDA *is*
barking at and discovers DEELUXE.)

MICHIGAN (*addressing Deeluxe's right hand*): I suppose you know what
this will mean. There will be no show. She will be unable to do the
show. You're not going to like this. (MICHIGAN *begins searching through*
the suit coats. She pulls out a phone receiver. Pink, plastic, sans cord—it
should be as phony looking as possible.) Hello? Ninth precinct? Yes, I'll
hold. (*To Deeluxe's hand:*) You're asking for this. (*To phone:*) There's
a man in here . . . I can't say if he's dangerous or not. I don't know any
other men so I can't compare . . . through the door! He lives with us.
More with her than with me. Me, this man, and the body . . . yes, there
certainly is a body . . . did I discover it? Many years ago. I first discovered the body in the Hotel Universal in Salamanca. A single light bulb.
The light came in through the window. The streets were lit by little
oranges. The oranges were perfect and bitter. In this light I lay down
on the bed and discovered the body. Especially the legs. She's part
palomino. In the legs, pure palomino. Do you know what a palomino
is? . . . a racehorse covered with Parmesan cheese, yes. That's her. And
after the first time I would discover the body again and again. And
even when I hate her, I love the body . . . who does the body belong
to? Partly to me. It belongs to her. I usually say she's my sister, and

most of the times we are sisters. Sometimes we're even worse . . . I don't know the address. I don't go out much. I don't go out at all, so I don't need an address. I could describe the place. We live in a town. I've forgotten the name. In the bad part of town. We live in a rental-clothing store. It doesn't look like much from the outside. But we have too many clothes for our own good. Is that enough of an address? Could you find us based on what I've just said? You're not there anymore, are you? She's not there anymore either. She's dead. Do you understand? Never mind, I understand. She probably won't be able to perform anymore. And I will never again lie down in the afternoon and discover the body. (MICHIGAN *replaces the phone in the suit coat. She begins speaking to* LINDA:) Is it cold in here or is it me? (*To* DEELUXE:) Oh, it's you. You should relax. You know there are worse things in New York than being killed by someone who loves you. Like trying to cash a check! Are you mad at me because I said your body belongs to me? (MICHIGAN *kneels down and opens Deeluxe's robe.*) Remember the night we became sisters? I looked out, and there were no more stars. The sky was full of teeth. Blue and sharp, and they were falling towards us. We were already in the wolf's mouth, and it was closing in around us.

Our only chance was to become twins. To be swallowed whole. But being twins slowed us down. People don't rent dress suits from twins.

But then there was always the body to come back to. I'm not going to look at you any longer. I got to look where I'm going. I never thought I would have to go anywhere. (MICHIGAN *crosses to the stereo and puts on a scratchy version of Frank Sinatra singing "A Lover Is Blue." While the record plays,* MICHIGAN *paces, drains her drink, and, looking at* DEELUXE, *polishes off hers as well. The stereo cuts off abruptly.* MICHIGAN *starts. A small wall sconce comes on. When* MICHIGAN *turns around to look at it, the light cuts off. The stereo comes on suddenly; it's the beginning bars of "Temptation," by Perry Como.* MICHIGAN *backs away from it. Deeluxe's dress falls off its hook.* MICHIGAN *stands still, afraid. Lights slowly cross-fade up—it's morning.* MICHIGAN *begins talking to* LINDA *again.*) Born in that cold-snap-spring-won't-come time of year. Under the sign of Go Fish. My Venus was stuck in the mud. Mud of the Bad River, she's acting up again.

Outgrowing her banks. Slipping through locked doors, spitting up coffins and dead Chevrolets. Leaving turds in the hope chest.

Stores running outta Bird's Eye frozen vegetables and everything plaid. People getting nervous they'd have to eat fresh food and wear solid colors. Thought the end of the world had come to Michigan. Nobody's hair would hold a set. Forsythia blooms so hard and sudden she cracks the plate-glass windows and then freezes all the way back to the ground.

And they blamed my mother. She was full of too much Bad River water. The end of the world, not spring, was coming to Michigan. And I was the first robin of disaster. When I started breathing on my own, the doctor went and beat me anyway, and Momma, she's screaming, "What is it? Is it a girl?"

And the doctor's screaming, "She's an animal!"

Animal, doc, you said it! I do the Rin-Tin-Tin: I get down on all fours. Being a girl is just a phase I'm going through. I feel my own ass up, and it's ticking like a time bomb. I am the end of the world after all.

Ticktock through the teacher's lounge where Mr. Science pins you against the wall in the name of higher learning. I like being pinned down, an' what do you think of that?

And he says, "I bet you wish you hadda father."

And I say, "Nope, I wish I had his clothes though," and I play with his tie, and he's screaming to stop it, oh, please stop it, but we don't stop it, we both want it till his tie is exploding in my hand like a trick cigar, and he slaps me hard and says: "You're an animal!"

Bomb on outta there. By now I'm sweating hard, and I break out in titties. See the girls in the hall, and my milk drops down. I got what they want and I wanna give it to them and I do. Right on the pink plastic floor. Ever seen a bunch a lamprey eels up close? Well, they're everywhere in Michigan now, and there're these girls too, their mouths are little oohs. Just made to suck. Go on, suck the life outta me, I wanna feel my life in somebody else's mouth.

Makes me know what Jesus feels. At communion. He feels good. We take communion to make Jesus feel better. Jesus feels like a big rare roast beef on a platter, squirting blood and fat on a platter and lifting his hips to heaven beggin' for it!: "Oh, God, yes! Yes, I need it, this is my body, hurry up and take it! Take me! Ketchup, mustard, and the Holy Ghost are with me! Please, God, oh, my God, oh, my God EAT ME!"

Then the girls get what they want, what we both want, and they stop being eels and go back to being girls again, and I'm just barely ticking when they slap me hard an' say: "You're an animal!"

I don't want nobody anymore. I wanna be by myself, just me and moon. I feel her before I see her. The moon pulls something tight in me. I get that ocean feeling. Ol' Michigan she was an ocean before she was anything else. A blue-green bottomless pit, that's what's in me. The moon she could be anything she wants. She's a bigger prize than you can win bowling; she's that white bread women keep between their legs. She's a mirror—I'm not afraid to look.

Oh, yoo-hoo! Mrs. Moon?

(*Piano music up, "Amato Mio." French windows swing open.*)

MICHIGAN: You're so smart and Italian. Tell me what I am.

(DEELUXE *begins to sit, opening a giant fan as she does. She's singing, "Amato Mio" à la Bela Lugosi, that is, with lots of rolling eyebrows. At the end of every phrase,* DEELUXE *strikes another pose against the fan. She looks like a singing art deco vase.* MICHIGAN *strikes poses of terror in unison with* DEELUXE. *At the song's end,* DEELUXE *picks up the illuminated tulips and offers them to the horrified* MICHIGAN.)

MICHIGAN: Why did you come back?

DEELUXE: The car.

MICHIGAN: The car?

DEELUXE: The keys!

MICHIGAN: They won't let you. Expired!

DEELUXE: Why? My license is good!

MICHIGAN: Not your license! You're no good. You're expired. They won't let a dead woman run around in a Chevrolet!

DEELUXE: I'm taking the Cadillac! Kiss me, and say you're sorry.

MICHIGAN: You'll make me sick! Your kisses are more ice water down my neck.

DEELUXE: You're my sister. I got rights.

MICHIGAN: I'm not your sister. I'm a White Christmas. I'm the wrong age for you. The age when you can't be sick. The Ice Age! Close the window.

> (DEELUXE *crosses and closes the window. She remains
> facing upstage, her back to* MICHIGAN.)

MICHIGAN: We need more sherry.

DEELUXE: I've had all I want.

MICHIGAN: We've exhausted the reserves.

DEELUXE: I'm sick of sherry.

MICHIGAN: There's money in the pocket.

DEELUXE: Is that a threat?

MICHIGAN: Get enough.

DEELUXE: I've had enough.

MICHIGAN: We need more.

DEELUXE: We? You! You need more. More of what?

MICHIGAN: You know.

DEELUXE: More of the same. More of the same conversations. More of the same air. Well, not me. I want.

MICHIGAN: What?

DEELUXE: I don't know. But it's not in this shop. It may not even be on this block. I may have to cross Second Avenue to get it. I know I don't want the same thing, because day after day I have the same thing, and at the end of the day I still want.

MICHIGAN: Hurry.

DEELUXE: You can't tell me what to do anymore. Well, I'm going. And I'm taking the money. (*Removes a piggy bank from a suit-coat pocket.*) Not for sherry. I'm getting what I want. (*Moves towards the exit.*) And if I come back—and I'm not saying that I will—I'm not telling you a thing. I need a secret. Well, my mind's made up. Nothing you can do or say can stop me. (*Pause.*) Well, this time I'm really going. Don't try to get in my way. Good-bye.

MICHIGAN: Go on.

DEELUXE (*turning around and recrossing the room*): I'm doing what I want, and I want to stay.

(DEELUXE *hunts through the boxes to find her clothes.*
She begins dressing. MICHIGAN *and* LINDA *observe.*)

DEELUXE: They said a lot of things about us. 'Cause of where we lived. You know that swamp. Used to be a river running through there, but the river got lost and turned belly up. Went dark and stinky, and we called it home.

Said we must be a lot like that lost river. Backed up. Scum. Living there in that place mutts went to die. Most people don't like mud. That's 'cause they don't know anything about it.

And they said we went to the Dairy Queen any chance we got. Just climbed outta the mud and went down and grabbed a Mr. Softee. But not them. Dairy Queen wasn't good enough for them. McDonald's crowd.

And that was just another reason for them to hate us. Us. Me and my mother, talk of the town. And my talk stank worse than their mud.

About my mother they said she wasn't a full-time woman. That other times she was a mud puppy and a river pussy. That we lived in quicksand and ate outta cans. That she had every single Petula Clark record and had to play them up full every night before she could get to sleep. That she looked right into men's crotches, and if she didn't like what she saw, she gave them a face full of her muddy spit.

Nasty talk about my mother. But it didn't hurt me none. Because it was all true. Every stinky last word of it, true. And the truth can't hurt you. Not if you're a young girl with mud on the brain.

And everywhere this young girl went the talk went too. Most of it about me and the new one. Me, you know my story by looking at me once. And her, that two-bit, small-town Pekinese. About her and me being lesbians. And that talk didn't hurt either. I coulda laughed. Lesbians. If it was that simple, that easy. Muff divers. They didn't know the half of it.

(DEELUXE *is fully dressed in her satin strapless gown.*
LINDA *begins barking in Michigan's lap.*)

MICHIGAN (*Placing* LINDA *on the floor*): What is it, Linda? You want to go out? You don't want to go out. I went out once. Five years ago. There's nothing out there. What do you smell? Pussy! No, Linda, no! No more pussy for us. That's just Little Peter. You know him, Little Peter from across the street. He had a nice thing going till he got his hands on that wildcat. No man can handle a wildcat. Nothing cuts as deep as mean pussy.

LITTLE PETER (*The character of* LITTLE PETER *is played by* DEELUXE. *From time to time he takes her over. When there are conversations between the two,* DEELUXE *speaks to her right hand, the place in her where* LITTLE PETER *lives.*): That's it. We're closed! Scram! Everybody but you sweetheart. (*To* DEELUXE:) Let me see your face. Hmmm. I like the eyes. Let's see the teeth. Nice. I like the face. But I don't like your song.

DEELUXE: Nobody likes it; that's why it's so good.

LITTLE PETER: Oooooh, honey, you're what's good.

DEELUXE: Deeluxe

LITTLE PETER (*slaps* DEELUXE): Guess again, sweetheart, you don't got a name. You don't need a name. You work for me now. Only name you got to remember is Little Peter. All you got to do is let him, love him. Let him touch your hair. How you make your hair do that? The way it comes out of your head like your brain's on fire. (*Little Peter's hand reaches for* DEELUXE, *who flinches.*) What started that fire in you? You can tell Little Peter.

MICHIGAN: That tiger was getting the best of Little Peter, and he didn't even know it. We just called her a tiger 'cause there weren't words for what she was. Half woman, half something weird. French, maybe. All cat.

LITTLE PETER: You think I want to hurt you? I want to be nice to you. It's you that makes me hurt you. You hurt yourself. Look at me. Not the eyes. At the hands. Don't the hands tell the truth? They want to be nice to you. Think of them as your own hands. Think of me as a part of you. Hmm, there. What's your name now?

DEELUXE: Deeluxe.

LITTLE PETER: Forget it! That part is over. Got it? Put some clothes on. Some, but not too many. And honey. I don't like girls who cry about their mother. Don't sing that song again.

MICHIGAN: Maybe I was as big a sucker as him. Even a dog's got sense to be afraid of cars. One look at her pelt, and I went stupid. Maybe I was as big a sucker as him. I knew what a hundred fifty pounds of killer pussy'd do to a man. What I didn't know is what it could do to a woman.

> (MICHIGAN *crosses to* DEELUXE. LITTLE PETER *seems to have settled down, but* DEELUXE *is wary of* MICHIGAN.)

MICHIGAN: We need more sherry to tide us over.

DEELUXE: You can see into the future, can't you?

MICHIGAN (*reaching for Deeluxe's right hand, the one controlled by* LITTLE PETER): Give me your hand.

DEELUXE: You know how it ends, don't you?

MICHIGAN: I need your hand.

DEELUXE: Why this hand?

MICHIGAN: That one you were born with, and this the one you made for yourself. Give.

DEELUXE: It's not mine to give.

MICHIGAN: What?

DEELUXE: It's not MY hand!

MICHIGAN: What could it be then?

DEELUXE: It could be anything. It works against me. I have no feeling in it. And it's not an "it." It's a he. He does what he wants and when he wants. He's an underground river that empties into my heart. I know what my heart is. It's a red whirlpool, and I got to watch so I don't fall in. And this hand is proof. Proof I was hit. Heat lightning. My own fault. Storms like trailer parks. I could never stay put when the pressure drops.

MICHIGAN: You look fine. (*Still trying to get the hand.*)

DEELUXE: I'm far from fine. I'm a tree, and I been hit bad. Still look like a tree on the outside, but on the inside there's just animals and disease and no tree left.

(MICHIGAN *is finally able to get Deeluxe's hand.*)

DEELUXE: What's he say?

MICHIGAN: He says your head line and your heart line split early on. He says you have a long life.

DEELUXE: How does it end?

MICHIGAN: It doesn't end really. Your life line runs into your veins.

DEELUXE: It's not forever I want!

MICHIGAN: Okay. It ends with you getting sherry.

DEELUXE: That's not how it ends. It ends with me leaving and never coming back! And then my life will start. You can't stop me!

(DEELUXE *crosses to the rack of tuxedos and begins
riffling through them as though she were going to get
dressed and leave.* MICHIGAN *watches without concern.*
DEELUXE *pulls an innocent-looking scarf out of a suit
pocket, but the scarf is a huge backdrop of a desert
scene. At this point, real time stops, that is, time stops
moving only forward. The following scene works in two
ways: as a flashback—à la Billy Pilgrim in* Slaughter-
house Five, *the characters become unstuck in time—
and also as a ritualistic reenactment of a past event.*
MICHIGAN *begins to loosen her robe, and* DEELUXE *pins
up the scarf-backdrop like a sheet hung out to dry.*)

DEELUXE: I'm going away.

(*In unison, the two begin to dress for the ritual.*
MICHIGAN *holds up a pair of pink high-heeled cowboy
boots as* DEELUXE *removes a pair of rhinestone earrings
with fetishistic attentiveness.* DEELUXE *picks up a tooth-
pick while* MICHIGAN *sticks a wad of bubble gum in her
mouth. They reach behind the hanging suits to pull out a
pair of Day-Glo hula hoops. As* MICHIGAN *begins to
cross downstage center,* DEELUXE *puts on a cowboy hat.*)

MICHIGAN (*addressing the audience and slinging her hoop*): Thirteen years old. Mama called me a woman and slapped me hard and gave me a silver dollar with a Bible verse: "Ask and you shall receive."

I put my Bible verse into the candy machine, pull hard, nada. Being good don't buy you sweet things anymore, I'm thinking when the foreign car pulls up and snake pops out. A real señor type a snake: cologne, real leather shoes coiling down the sidewalk. No offer a candy, just gives me one hard bite and he's off. Greases back his hair with mother's milk and takes off with those other too-handsome kind a guys.

Nothing showed on the outside, but I was bleeding bad on the inside. Skin goes the color of flophouse sheets. Poison's working on me and all I wanted was some more poison. Mama taught us to feed a fever, and I got a hot python squeezing that little girl's heart. All that sugar and spice running down my legs and staining up those spanky pants. My heart was sweating and contagious with that secret dirt, and I ripped those panties off and went without underwear. Hoping for an accident and soon. Poison's gotta work itself outta you, and the only way outta you is into somebody else.

Felt like touching my new wound but didn't dare. Knew somebody would lose a finger in there, and it wasn't gonna be me. Disguised myself with a cross around my neck and a kilt on, too. Let that skirt ride up, and my bare ass rose like a wet moon over the candy store.

Snake on down to the mall. Coiling and uncoiling in the dust. Looking for somebody to infect. Poison's gotta work itself out. Staring at all those girls that never got bit. The blonde that would bring out the blonde in me. Take my sweet meat out behind the cheap shoe stores and lay her down in the AstroTurf and make her mine. Carve my initials on the insides a her thigh with my tongue. Gonna give her a little scar to remember me by, gonna match mine.

I'm shaking, I'm rattling, baby needs a new way to sing the blues, come on, come on, let's go, snake eyes.

(MICHIGAN *drops her hoop. Music up: it's the instrumental theme from* A Man and a Woman. DEELUXE *crosses to center stage moving as much like a cowboy as you can in a strapless gown and heels.* DEELUXE *snaps her hula hoop over to* MICHIGAN *so that it rolls past her, then boomerangs back.* MICHIGAN *catches it. Music fades out as they begin to speak.*)

MICHIGAN: Fill 'er up?

DEELUXE: Just five dollars, thanks.

MICHIGAN: Oil okay? Water? Small engine.

DEELUXE: Checked it this morning in Tulsa.

MICHIGAN: Oh, the big city, huh? And they didn't tell you about me in Tulsa? They didn't tell you this was your last chance?

DEELUXE: Every place on this road says that.

MICHIGAN: Well, I am flattered. You know what they say about imitation! Everyone wanting a piece of my action. Maybe they can sucker a few but they can't improve on reality. Believe me, I've tried. I'm the only real thing for fifty miles around. I'm it. I'm the end of the line.

DEELUXE: Okay, keep the change; just give me the keys.

MICHIGAN: Just where do you think you going in such an all-fired hurry? California?

DEELUXE: So what?

MICHIGAN: California! Watcha gonna do in Cala . . . ha, ha . . . fornia?

DEELUXE: Look around.

MICHIGAN: Oh, there's a lot to see out there in California, all right. Man-size mice dancing with movie stars with missile-sized tits. Or is it tit-sized missiles? Two-stepping through the mud slides. No, you sure don't want to miss that. You'll never make it.

DEELUXE: I'm gonna see California.

MICHIGAN: You're gonna see California, but you're not leaving this station. 'Cause I already seen California, and I'm gonna show you my shots. I got all the best places. (*Begins to display her tattoos as though they were souvenirs.*)

DEELUXE: Disneyland? Knott's Berry Farm? Universal Studios? Marineland? (*Her hand is resting on Michigan's crotch.*)

MICHIGAN: Sorry about Marineland. Dropped my camera into the killer-whale tank. Didn't dare go in after it. Sharks are terrified of me. Are you ready to see California?

> (A Man and a Woman *theme music up.* DEELUXE *takes out her toothpick as* MICHIGAN *spits her gum into her hand. They kiss. After the kiss, they replace the tooth- pick and gum. Music fades as they begin to speak.*)

DEELUXE: So that's California, huh?

MICHIGAN: Yeah.

DEELUXE: So we should do something.

MICHIGAN: So?

DEELUXE: Why stay here?

MICHIGAN: So what, and just because.

DEELUXE: That's what I thought.

MICHIGAN: So what if I got no friends and no money. There's no snakes here. I could go some place and get friends and money, but then I might get snakes. Besides, my nothing is better than your something.

DEELUXE: Well, I was just thinking . . .

MICHIGAN: Don't start. Just shut up and be happy. (*Picks up her hula hoop and begins to rattle it.*)

DEELUXE: What's that?

MICHIGAN: A snake.

DEELUXE: You promised no snakes!

(MICHIGAN *slips the hoop over Deeluxe's head.*)

MICHIGAN: Quick!

DEELUXE: What?

MICHIGAN: Here!

DEELUXE: How?

MICHIGAN: Suck.

(*They kiss. The hoop drops.*)

MICHIGAN: I'm beginning to like this desert air. So refreshing. (*Pause.*) You spit it out, didn't you?

DEELUXE: What?

MICHIGAN: The poison.

DEELUXE: What poison?

MICHIGAN: My poison. You spit it out?

DEELUXE: I swallowed it.

(MICHIGAN *crosses upstage and begins folding up the backdrop.* DEELUXE *faces the audience.*)

DEELUXE: She's got a bad heart. The kind you die from. Runs in the family. I gotta bad heart too. Just not the kind you die from. The kind that makes you wear too much eye makeup.

She's my cousin, comes up from one of those sweaty states. She wouldn't sweat in a forest fire. Ice wouldn't melt in her mouth. I make a little bet with myself. I can make her sweat.

The first time I know for sure I got heart problems is when my cousin came to visit. Heat spell. Bad heart and bad heat spell couldn't keep my cousin from pitching pop-ups in the garden. Takes everything she has and makes it into a ball. Something in me follows that ball up, and it hangs in the air a moment, seems like forever, then into the dirt.

I can't throw, can't make a fist. She can throw and stay cool. She's a little bit Catholic. So yellow, her hair, it hurts my teeth. I sneak her weenies on Friday, and I don't tell on her forbidden patent leathers, hoping they'll reflect up to that place she's got muscles girls don't, got heart places boys don't. Don't want to do nothing about it yet; still that bad heart of mine wanna bite.

She's still not sweating, but I get to sleep with her because there's not enough beds. I iron my father's shorts and bleach his stains to send her roses.

Downstairs with her, the fake wood, the pump straining to keep us from going under. The earth sweating through the fake wood. Lip-synching to forty-fives. I got the aspirins, she got the cokes, waiting for it to happen. And the sweat is all over us now, hers and mine together tasting like a memory of a place I never been. Waiting for it to happen, for one heart to give out, for the rattler to strike.

(LITTLE PETER *begins to invade* DEELUXE. *Her hand begins twitching and, finally, singing:*)

LITTLE PETER:

> *She may be weary,*
> *Women do get weary,*
> *Wearing the same shabby dress.*
> *And when she's weary,*
> *Try a little tenderness.*

(*To* DEELUXE:) Yeah, go on and try it, sucker, see what it'll get you.

DEELUXE: I can do it.

LITTLE PETER: We aren't talking about an "it" here to do. We are talking skirt, a woman, a Jane.

DEELUXE: So?

LITTLE PETER: So you don't do a woman. You handle her.

DEELUXE: Like you used to handle me, huh?

LITTLE PETER: Correction, carrot brain, like I did, do, and will handle you.

DEELUXE: Stay outta this.

LITTLE PETER: I'll sit out this fox-trot, but I'll be around.

> (DEELUXE *crosses to* MICHIGAN *and takes off*
> *Michigan's hat.*)

DEELUXE: I'm back. I'm sorry.

MICHIGAN: No, you're not.

DEELUXE: I know you said you wanted to be alone.

MICHIGAN: Did I?

DEELUXE: You said I shouldn't see you again.

> (MICHIGAN *starts laughing.*)

DEELUXE: What's so funny?

MICHIGAN: You should laugh. Be happy. I thought tall people laughed a lot.

DEELUXE: What about?

MICHIGAN: About me being such a liar. I didn't want to be alone. Did you want me to be alone?

DEELUXE: No.

MICHIGAN: And wouldcha leave me alone?

DEELUXE: No.

MICHIGAN: Until?

DEELUXE: No until. I won't leave.

MICHIGAN: Period?

DEELUXE: Period.

MICHIGAN: Wouldcha leave if I asked you to go?

DEELUXE: I would try.

MICHIGAN: You would?

DEELUXE: If you asked.

MICHIGAN: Oh.

DEELUXE: But I couldn't leave.

MICHIGAN: Well, if you can't leave, then I guess you can stay. (*Starts laughing.*)

DEELUXE: This time it's really not funny.

MICHIGAN: Show me. Make me stop laughing if you don't like it.

DEELUXE (*addressing her* LITTLE PETER *hand*): Help me. I don't know what to do.

MICHIGAN (*singing*):

> *You won't regret it,*
> *Women don't forget it,*
> *Love is their whole happiness.*

Aren't you glad I stuck around? Okay, now let's try a little tenderness.

> (DEELUXE *displays an invisible key to* MICHIGAN. *Then*
> *she mimes locking the door with it and swallowing*
> *the key. It's as though her entire body were taken over*
> *by* LITTLE PETER.)

LITTLE PETER: Did you see what I did with that key?

MICHIGAN: So what?

LITTLE PETER: That's what I'm going to do to you.

MICHIGAN: Huh?

LITTLE PETER: I'm gonna swallow you whole. There's a part of you no-body sees. A part I know is there. Like I know what white stuff is in the middle of those black cookies. But you gotta twist open the whole rotten thing to get to it. (*Begins caressing* MICHIGAN *more fiercely than tenderly.*) That's what I'm gonna do to you. It's your secret now, but I'm going to know it too. Make your cream the glue between us. No matter what it costs me. Or you. (*Yanks* MICHIGAN *to her feet.*)

MICHIGAN: Aren't you afraid?

DEELUXE: No.

MICHIGAN: You should be. You're lucky you're so dumb.

DEELUXE: You're afraid.

MICHIGAN: Of what? I'm the scariest thing going.

DEELUXE: There's something even worse.

MICHIGAN: Yeah?

DEELUXE: The cold.

MICHIGAN: What's that? I ain't been cold a day in my life. You afraid?

DEELUXE: Yes, I got no feeling anywhere.

MICHIGAN: So?

DEELUXE: So I could die and not even notice it.

(*French windows blow open. Howling wind is heard.*)

MICHIGAN: Shut it!

DEELUXE: You shut it!

MICHIGAN: You're closer.

DEELUXE: Closer to what?

MICHIGAN: The window.

DEELUXE: I wasn't talking about the window!

   (MICHIGAN *closes the window. Howling stops.*)

DEELUXE: I thought you were hot enough for both of us. I guess I was wrong.

MICHIGAN: I got the heat, sweetheart; I just don't give it away. (*Pulls a long, black flashlight out of a suit-coat pocket.*)

DEELUXE: What's that for?

MICHIGAN: Stars.

DEELUXE: It's aimed down at the street. That's a funny place to look for stars. There's no stars on this part of Second Avenue. Just three bums pissing on a futon. Hey! You can see right into my bedroom! You been looking at me!

MICHIGAN: No.

DEELUXE: Yes, you have. This is proof.

MICHIGAN: I been more than looking. I been watching. That's looking with a reason.

DEELUXE: What's the reason?

MICHIGAN: 'Cause you're my kind of star.

DEELUXE: What's that?

MICHIGAN: A falling star. Wanna see one? It's a nice night for viewing. Rare to see so many binaries.

DEELUXE: Binaries?

MICHIGAN: Doubles. A pair of stars so close they cannot escape each other.

DEELUXE: Close as sisters?

MICHIGAN: Closer. Like twins.

DEELUXE: How come they stay together?

MICHIGAN: Gravity.

DEELUXE: I don't see anything like that.

MICHIGAN: And the closer they get, the worse it gets.

DEELUXE: What?

MICHIGAN: The pull, and then it's . . . kaboom. But there's that moment right before the end when they're the brightest thing on Second Avenue. Just a big red nova.

DEELUXE: I had one of those once. Not fancy but a good car.

MICHIGAN: Course, even the brightest star can get stuck with a black hole.

DEELUXE: What's that?

MICHIGAN: Something so dense you can't imagine it. You wait and wait, and the bang you counted on never comes.

DEELUXE: Is that what makes a star fall?

MICHIGAN: Almost anything can make a star fall. Here's one now, about to fall.

> (MICHIGAN *directs Deeluxe's flashlight so it shines on herself. Throughout the following monologue,* MICHIGAN *strikes different peep-show poses while* DEELUXE *observes her as attentively but asexually as a nerd looking at an ant farm.*)

DEELUXE: I see it. Looks familiar. Looks like me. That was the year I was living alone in Bad Axe. Just wouldn't move in with him. "What's the difference?" he'd say.

   Then he'd go off and leave me trying to decide whether to be a lesbian today or put it off till tomorrow.

   And then I'd put on plastic nurse's shoes. Wait on tables. Getting tips in Bible verses. People with one eye ate at this place a lot. I guess it was just about the favorite place of one-eyed people to eat. Down at the mall. Not even a real mall, fucking shopping center.

   One day I get up with him, and alla sudden I'm falling. And I tried to break my fall by reaching out for him. But it didn't come out that way. I socked him once, twice in the jaw and kept falling. Falling into the Chevy with the bad plates with a cat and a raincoat. I don't know what started it, and what I'm falling into.

MICHIGAN (*directing flashlight so it falls on her own breasts*): Probably the moon.

DEELUXE: I dunno. Is the moon that strong?

MICHIGAN: Take a look and see.

DEELUXE: Wow. Get a load of that moon. She's so full. There's two moons, and they're both full.

MICHIGAN: Don't tell me she's not strong enough to pull you off course. (*Takes the flashlight out of Deeluxe's hands.*)

DEELUXE: What's going on here?

MICHIGAN: I got nothing to hide. (*Grabs Deeluxe's bodice.*) What about you?

DEELUXE: Don't get me naked. I get so Italian when I'm naked.

MICHIGAN: Thought you wanted that secret. Wanna touch it? Touch me the way you touch him.

DEELUXE: I don't!

MICHIGAN: Don't lie. Just tell me you love me.

DEELUXE: I can't say that.

MICHIGAN (*wrapping* DEELUXE *in the strand of pearls*): There, does that make it any easier?

> (*The two are bound together and begin a slow
> circle dance.*)

MICHIGAN: Soon as they start to shine, they start to change. The center contracts. Pressure at the center rises. And the center can't hold up.

> (DEELUXE *backs away. The pearls break.* DEELUXE *and*
> MICHIGAN *face each other for a long beat. Then* DEELUXE
> *turns away.* MICHIGAN *sinks to the floor and begins
> picking up the pearls.*)

MICHIGAN: You take care of something, it grows. You can see I got the knack. Too big? Is there such a thing as "too big"? Besides, it's just the way I am. Too damned juicy for my own good. With you around it gets wicked. One look at you, and my pink pulp starts pounding.

(DELUXE *begins to unzip her gown*.)

MICHIGAN: Wanna know something? They're gonna get bigger. That pink is gonna go all the way into red. Then you watch out. My sap's running from the heat of your eyes. That special blue heat outta the eyes gets the pink ocean stirred up. That's when you squeeze them. Put the muscle on those peaches till my bucks are bucking like I'm riding an invisible palomino.

(DELUXE *is in her underwear, black tap pants and a corset. She reaches out for* MICHIGAN.)

MICHIGAN: Well, I dunno, I might let you. These peaches getting mighty tight. But I gotta decide. What you ever done for me except make me cry? Right now I'm sobbing bad. Just look, I'm crying for you. You look hungry. Come on, get it, squeeze it outta me, suck it outta me. I wanna be totally Spain when you're done with me.

(MICHIGAN *begins to put on a filmy peignoir as she sings the following song. Her actions are as flirtatious as if she were stripping.* MICHIGAN *sings*:)

Bugs are bitin',
Fish are jumpin'
When my baby starts a humpin' me.
Hot cross buns
Always beg for jam.
Every beaver
Needs a beaver dam.
Taste of fish,
Taste of chicken,
Don't taste like the girl I'm lickin'.
She puts the cunt back in country,
Pulls the rug out from under me.
In case you are wondering,
She can put what she wants in me.

Hot sweet cream
Dripping from my pet.
How I scream
When she gets me wet
With her finger
On my sugarplum.
There she lingers
Till I start to come
'Cause she puts the cunt back in country,
Pulls the rug out from under me.
In case you are wondering,
She can put what she wants in me.

(DEELUXE *is tired of the tease. She dons a black tuxedo*
jacket. It's a magician's jacket. There are scarves, paper
flowers, etcetera, in the pockets. During the following
monologue, DEELUXE *fumbles with the jacket, and the*
objects seem to fly from her pockets. DEELUXE *faces*
the audience.)

DEELUXE: A lotta people ask me: "What about Ohio?" And I have to tell them what I know. Because I'm part buckeye.

Not that you would know. That's why I never take all my clothes off all at the same time, so you can never see the Ohio in me. But I haven't forgotten about Toledo, and I won't. The very mention of the word "Toledo" makes me wanna puke.

Toledo used to belong to us. We went to war to save it. People always ask: "Why'd you bother to have a war in Toledo? Aren't the winters there war enough?" Things got pretty bad between me and Toledo, and a pig was killed. The government came in like they always do, but the fighting went on when no one was looking. They took away Toledo. Gave us this little chunk of perpetual January that used to belong to Minnesota.

Don't even get me started about Minnesota.

When everybody else is dead, I'm going to get a nice slab of Ohio. Right now it's my Uncle Bert's asparagus patch. I hate asparagus. I'm afraid of it. Especially at night when the stalks look like dead people from Toledo giving you the finger.

We'd take these trips to visit the land. Going as fast as we could, pretending to be going someplace else. I guess that's the only way to live through a trip to Ohio: Pretend to be going someplace else. And keep the window rolled up tight. Ohio air can make you dizzy if you're not used to it. Remember: in the winters here they set the rivers on fire.

We get to the land, and they break out the asparagus and put on the ham. Aunt Helen is fat, and she waits on the skinny people. We do things that way in Ohio: the fat people wait on the skinny ones. Course, everyone in my family is fat. Except for Bert. But then he's not one of us. The only reason they let him stay in Ohio is he porked Aunt Helen back in that freak thaw last leap year.

After dinner Bert helps Helen up the stairs. I do the dishes, and they do it. When a three-hundred-and-fifty-pound woman has sex in a wood-frame house in Ohio, you know about it. Bert liked to get her right after the ham when she still had mayonnaise on her arms.

Helen died before Bert learned what to do about asparagus. He just went out back and lay down in the mud. Face down. We left him that way. Very polite.

And then I read in this magazine about this man that loves mud. Loves it better than he loves his dead wife. "Mud is better than any woman. You don't have to wait till after dinner. And it's romantic. After a rain. During a sunset. You just find a place and stick it in."

And the letter was signed. Bert from Ohio. And that's Ohio.

(MICHIGAN *crosses to the stereo and puts on a record—*
"Temptation." They do a tango that ends with
MICHIGAN *dipping* DEELUXE. *Suddenly,* LITTLE PETER
appears and begins talking to DEELUXE. MICHIGAN
watches the dialogue like someone watches a seizure or a
crazy on an IRT.)

LITTLE PETER: We gotta talk.

DEELUXE: Leave me alone.

LITTLE PETER: Alone, who's alone? You're not alone. You probably couldn't even spell it. Always had me on your side. Don't sleep alone. Don't take a shit alone. Little Peter holds your hand. I seen alone, and it's not for you. Maybe I know the wrong kind of alone. You wanna be alone all right, alone with her.

DEELUXE (to MICHIGAN): Would you like some more sherry?

(MICHIGAN shakes her head no.)

LITTLE PETER: Why don't you ask her if she wants to be alone with you? Maybe she'd like a chaperon. Go ahead, ask her.

DEELUXE: I'm not going to ask her.

LITTLE PETER: Maybe she'd like me better, huh?

DEELUXE: She won't like you. She can't see you.

LITTLE PETER: She can see me. You're the one who can't see me.

DEELUXE: We're over. I'm not talking to you anymore.

LITTLE PETER: What?

DEELUXE: I said I'm not talking to you anymore. You're not real.

LITTLE PETER: You're doing it, sister. Not real. What kinda thing is that to say to a friend? Hey, if I'm not real, what does that make you?

DEELUXE: Keep your hands off me.

LITTLE PETER: Deeluxe, please!

DEELUXE: One minute. Just one. But don't go touching me. (*To* MICHIGAN:) There's this guy I know, um—outside. He's outside. That's why you can't see him. I gotta go give him some money. I'll be right back. (DEELUXE *crosses to the stage right window and pulls down the shade. The area is backlit so her shadow appears. The* LITTLE PETER *hand comes out from behind the shade. Deeluxe's hand follows, grabs* LITTLE PETER, *and "strangles" him. After the* LITTLE PETER *hand is limp,* DEELUXE *crosses to* MICHIGAN.) You got to show them. They never believe you till you show them.

MICHIGAN: Is he gone?

DEELUXE: He's gone. Don't think about him. (*Pause.*) What you looking at?

MICHIGAN: You.

DEELUXE: Quit it.

MICHIGAN: You quit it.

DEELUXE: Me? What am I doing? It's not coming from me. I heard about you. What you do to women, what you make other women do. I'm not going to let you do that to me. I'm going to open the window and cry for help. I'm going to get the National Guard, the Marines, the *New York Times*, the Weight Watchers. I'm going to tell the world that evil is alive and well, and living on Second Avenue. I'm going to—

> (*French windows blow open. Sound of howling wind.*
> MICHIGAN *stands up and crosses stage left. She puts on a fox-fur stole. It's a larger, more gory version of the type with the head clipped on to the tail.*)

MICHIGAN: Tell me again. What are you going to do? That's what I thought you were going to do. Nothing! And what did you say you thought I was? Tell me.

DEELUXE: You. You're an animal.

MICHIGAN: And what do you think you are? A fucking zucchini?

DEELUXE: Stop. Why don't you stop?

MICHIGAN: Because you don't want me to stop.

DEELUXE: I could make you.

MICHIGAN: Go ahead. Make me.

DEELUXE: Cross the line.

MICHIGAN: I already crossed that line a long time ago. And this line. Go on, honey. Do it to me. Do it to me before I cross this line too.

DEELUXE: That's enough.

MICHIGAN: Sure it is. When you're really good, you don't have to touch. She walks in the room, and you don't touch. You don't even talk. But you feel her on every inch of your body like a suit of clothes you put on and can't take off. Feels like silk. But tight. Like a silk straitjacket. You're in deep and getting deeper. It's like being buried alive. And you like it.

DEELUXE: I won't . . .

(DEELUXE *attempts to exit, but* MICHIGAN *grabs her breast.*)

MICHIGAN: There's nothing you won't do. This is what you wanted all along, and no one has to know. It'll be our secret.

DEELUXE: What will?

MICHIGAN: Our secret will be what makes you tick.

> (*Deeluxe's bodice rips. Pearls and magic flowers explode
> out of it as* DEELUXE *breaks away from* MICHIGAN.)

DEELUXE:

> *I was never right.*
> *Look into my eyes,*
> *See the trouble,*
> *See the fire under water,*
> *See my brain's too big,*
> *See my heart's too small,*
> *I gotta pump it,*
> *That's why I gotta pump it.*
>
> *I tried to make my heart move another way,*
> *But the blood's too thin,*
> *Like the see-through blouse*
> *Momma puts on when Daddy leaves the house.*
> *My body's too fat like Crisco in the pan.*
> *It smokes, it steams, it cries out for meat.*
> *There's no other way your ham sure hits my spot,*
> *And if that don't grease the clock,*
> *You gotta pump it.*
>
> *I call my private Jesus on the pay telephone,*
> *Down on my knees in a booth filled with piss,*
> *Asking the King o' Love, won'tcha please*
> *Strike me dead.*
> *I can't live a life with a head too big,*
> *I can't get a laugh with a shrunken love pump.*

My too-big head's filled with a too-bad thought.
It stinks, it bites, it goes straight to the brain
Till I pump it.

It's not just bad,
It's more than bad it's wrong,
In the wrong place.
My heart got stuck between my legs.
You wouldn't think, I wouldn't think,
Such a tiny thing could put the muzzle on the brain
On those full-moon nights the way it beats so bad
No top forty drum machine,
More a solo with a shake.

I gotta bad heart, but I'm a nice girl, girl.
I'm not a girl at all, I'm more like a car.
A nice new car, why don't you thumb me down.
I'll let you take the wheel.

A woman with a bad heart gets lonely when she drives herself insane.
Take the wheel, and I'll let you bite my ham.
Turn the key over quick, put your boot to the floor.
If you don't get the power first,
Gotta pump it.

MICHIGAN: I'm getting out of here!

DEELUXE: I'm dying, you can't do that! Rip somebody's heart out and leave them to die!

MICHIGAN: I do it all the time.

DEELUXE: Then it's true!

MICHIGAN: Yes, it's true, let me go!

DEELUXE: If you go, I'll die.

MICHIGAN: If I stay, you'll be worse than dead. You'll be like me.

DEELUXE: What are you? (*Collapses.*)

MICHIGAN: There's a word for it in Michigan. From the early days of Michigan. Before Michigan was Motown or Ford four doors or Gerald Ford or Chevy hatchbacks and before the soybeans, sweet cherries, and mint fields went in. Before they started burning the sugar beets and soaking the kirbies in barrels of brine. Before they opened the Keewanah for copper pennies.

Before all that, when all Michigan was cold. Mooneye, steelhead, alewife, all of that. A coupla shriveled spits of land shivering in glacial puddles that'd lost their salt, that's what Michigan was. All she grew was protection from the cold. Beaver protection, and weasel, fisher, marten, mink, red fox, gray fox, catamount, muskrat, lynx, and bobcat too. Fur. Pelts.

And all of a sudden, Michigan was full of Frenchmen. They set their trap lines out on the ice. Along the Manistee, the Ausable. But the animals they caught didn't die right away. They lay out on the ice freezing and snarling and bleeding until the stars, most of them, fled to Canada.

And Orion bent down out of the January sky and put a silver bullet in their brains. Silver on the brain, they changed. Became monsters out on that ice. Until the Frenchmen came back, and the monsters became hats. Fancy hats and pocketbooks.

But there was something else out there. Another sort of animal. Or a woman. They always called her a "she." She came along the trap lines before the Frenchmen. She ripped open the steel and tossed it into the Tittabawassee. She set free the monsters.

Whatever she was, she had a mean head on her shoulders, shaped like a wedge of Pinconning extra-sharp cheddar cheese gone bad and a fat ass. She was always about fifty-six years old. And the monsters crashed through the split-level prefab houses of the Frenchmen and fucked their wives and got them full of baby monsters.

They don't say this anymore in Michigan. No one knows what happened to the woman who set the monsters free. The woman who was an animal. Loup-garou.

They said that women were monsters. Because they had teeth in their parts. And now they say we're not like that. We're not dangerous anymore.

But it's a lie. We are monsters. We got teeth in our parts, and we're so hungry. If you stay here, I'll eat you alive. Do you understand? Do you still want to be like me?

(MICHIGAN *turns upstage and crosses to hang up the*
fur. While MICHIGAN *is still turned upstage,* DEELUXE
slowly sits up.)

MICHIGAN: Why did you come back?

DEELUXE: I live here.

MICHIGAN: Lived here. I liked it when you were dead, because I got to do all the things I always wanted to but you kept me from doing.

DEELUXE: Like what?

MICHIGAN: Redecorate.

DEELUXE: It's the same.

MICHIGAN: It's not the same.

(DEELUXE *moves towards* MICHIGAN, *who is seated.*)

MICHIGAN: This is my chair.

DEELUXE (*sitting down in her chair*): I only been gone five minutes.

(*A blue airmail letter falls out of the skylight.* MICHIGAN
rushes to pick it up, then hands it to DEELUXE.)

MICHIGAN: It's for you.

DEELUXE (*reading the letter*): "Dear Deeluxe,
    You asked about the future. Here's the deal: it's gonna be just
like the past. In the past the heart of the world was filled with carbon
and water, and that is why we had life on earth. When everything got
heavier, the world started collapsing in on itself, an old heart in a fat
body. Aunt Helen collapsing in Cleveland. After the baby was born.
The one who couldn't talk. Or get up to go to the bathroom by herself. And Aunt Helen, she just collapsed. Carbon and water into dia-
monds. And in the future, women will replace the world. In a woman's
heart there is rice and water, and that is why there is life on earth. But
in the future, women will start collapsing the world thick with babies
who can't talk and only daughters who live alone on Oreos. And rice
and water will be crushed into tears. But no one will cry. The tears
will stay inside. They will be the hardest things known to man.
Women's tears will be used. In the future, women's tears will put a
man on the moon. And in the future, all the men who kill for a living
will wear pinky rings with women's tears.
    Love always,
    Little Peter."
    (*Pause.*) So that's the future, huh?

MICHIGAN (*pouring sherry for a toast*): Don't worry. We'll never see it.

(MICHIGAN STARTS TO RAISE HER GLASS TO DEELUXE'S BUT THE
UPSTAGE WINDOW SHADE FLIES UP. THERE IS A HAND AT THE WIN-
DOW WITH A PINKY RING. DEELUXE AND MICHIGAN CONTINUE STARING
AT THE HAND AS THE LIGHTS FADE DOWN AND OUT.)

THE END

World without
End

My mother wanted to burn.

Before she taught me anything else—how to insert a tampon without ruining yourself for your husband; how to tell if a man liked butter, and what to do if he didn't; how to make the most of any meat—before I learned any of that, my mother told me what to do with her body after she died. She wanted to be cremated.

This wasn't something that she happened to mention casually. I didn't figure out she preferred cremation, because of some off-hand comment made after another's funeral. It was something she told my sister and me over and over, speaking slowly and carefully because we were still so little, and what she was saying was just too important for us to get wrong. Important not only to her but to us, too: "You're going to have to make sure it happens. I'll know if you don't. I'll come back to haunt you."

She asked us if we understood. How could we not? And this is what we knew: My mother was going to die, and when she did, her body would belong to us. So much of our lives would depend on what we did with her death. After she was gone, there would still be her body, a light, a small fire still burning in the middle of our lives.

I never asked myself: where is my father? Even as a kid I could read the distance between my parents and know there was just no way he could be counted on to make her burn.

After my mother died, my sister and I made sure she had exactly the kind of burial she had wanted. But her body wouldn't go away. She couldn't burn completely; to burn completely she would have had to have started burning much earlier, when she was still alive. Not that she hadn't wanted to. There were at least two kinds of flames she wanted to jump into. She wanted to be an artist, and she wanted to have sex. But she just couldn't figure out how to burn like that and stay alive. She knew the middle-class life she was used to could never withstand that much heat.

After my mother died . . . well, after my mother died, all of my sentences began with "after my mother died . . . " But there was something besides her body that wouldn't go away. Burning questions I had about what it meant to be a lesbian, what it meant to be white. I had this carefully constructed identity by then, and I avoided the questions just as I had once stepped over the broken pavement that could have hurt my mother. I wondered how lesbian scholars who were always talking about how identities were socially constructed would react when I started taking mine apart right before their very eyes. And how much heat could I take. I wrapped my arms around my mother's body, and my questions and I jumped into the flames. *World without End* is the record of how we burned.

****

An overstuffed wingback chair upstage right, facing the audience. A small end table is placed to the left of the chair. On the table is a china vase filled with flowers. The flowers could be anything seasonal and old-fashioned, say, peonies or big, juicy mums. Roses would be fabulous, of course, if you can afford them. Just to the left and slightly downstage of the end table is a huge pot of hydrangeas.

Blackout. In the darkness a woman enters. The audience can hear her heels clicking on the floor. She is carrying a composition book, which she tosses onto the chair.

Lights up, a special on the chair area. Make it flattering. The woman is seated on the floor behind the chair, with her back to the audience. A leg sticks out on either side of the chair. During the following section, the woman

speaks with a steely sort of calm. She is laying her cards
on the table; she has just recently crossed some personal
Rubicon. She gestures with her hands as she speaks.

Okay. Here's the deal.
I'm going to tell you a story. It's just a little story.
Nothing heavy. A story about a bird.
But the thing is, right now I can't remember the name of the bird!

Jesus. What was the name of that bird?
All I remember is: she had a nest under the eaves.
She was very ordinary looking. You know. Small. Brown.
And I don't remember seeing the male around very much.
But she came back. Every year. The *same bird.*
Okay, so maybe it wasn't exactly the same bird as when I was a kid!
But it could have been her daughter.
It could have even been her daughter's daughter.
So the thing is: some nights my father would come home drunk.
There'd be the sounds of insults. Screams. Breaking glass.
You know. The usual family stuff, right?
And I'd open the window very carefully because she might have a
          family.
And I'd look at that nest.
Sure looked like a piece of shit to me.
But she came back. Every year.
That could mean this was a safe place after all.
Or it could mean she didn't know any better.
She didn't know what else to do except go on living in the mess her
          mother made.
We don't know. We don't even know her name.
I bet my mother does, though.
I'm going to ask her when I get a chance.
She is still calling me! Can you believe it? I mean—look at me.
I'm completely grown-up, and she is dead.
What's there to say about it?

Get over it, Mom.

Hey, if she calls tonight, will you answer the phone, please?

Will you ask her for me: What is the name of that bird?

Don't worry. She'll know the one I was talking about.

We only had one bird in our family.

> (*Blackout. Lights up. The woman is sitting in the chair.*
> *Sitting, what am I saying? She's lounging. One leg is*
> *draped over the side; she's sunk deep into the cushions.*
> *She's wearing a red silk off-the-shoulder number,*
> *possibly her mother's, and gold high heels. She's just*
> *stepped out of a Balthus painting. The composition book*
> *is open on her lap, and she reads from it.*)

What could I have been thinking about?

Nothing. I wasn't thinking; I was *cooking*. I didn't have a phone. Whenever Mom would start calling around for me, I'd just get out the big knife. Start chopping up everything I could get my hands on. Everything that wasn't nailed down.

He'd just laugh. Roll a joint. You see, he was a prep cook. Me? I was just short-order. He really knew his way around a kitchen. He had a respect for vegetables I didn't understand at the time.

I don't think he knew I had a mother. I never told him. I certainly didn't tell him I had a girlfriend. Well, I used to.

Look, I don't think there's anything wrong in me paying for her abortion. I mean, I was the one who loved her, not him.

But after the third one! All I wanted to do was *cook*.

She was a vegetarian, so I just made sure I was up to my elbows in chopped meat. In case she'd come looking for me. I'd go into the walk-in, and he'd ask: "Need a hand?"

And I'd say: "No. *This is something I have to do for myself.*"

I'd see those big cardboard cartons full of frozen beef patties, and I'd rip into them. With my bare hands. I'd lift out the pink beef Frisbees, crack them apart on the counter, and zing them into the broiler. I would have preferred to fry them, but he wouldn't let me.

I'm the one responsible here.

I followed him out to the cellar one night. The ground was soft and uneven, and I almost lost him. But I found him again. With my mouth. I kissed him. Not knowing I was going to do it until I was already doing it. His mouth was cool and closed at first. But then it grew. It opened. And I thought, of course, about flowers.

Then out of nowhere came the smell of roses, invisible!

Who planted these flowers? I knew they couldn't be wild. I thought I was going to fall. So I put my arms around him. But he kept his arms folded to his chest. I noticed his arms were full of tomatoes.

"Careful," he said. "Easy. These tomatoes are from my mother's garden."

(She tosses her composition book away, leans forward, and speaks to the audience.)

I think we should start now, okay?

(She turns and looks at the vase on the end table. She's annoyed by it, and grabbing the flowers, she throws them over her shoulder and then takes a nice long drink of water. From the vase. Her legs are spread. She wipes her mouth with the back of her hand. She picks out people in the audience in the following section. If this is to be done in some fancy-schmancy sort of theater, you know, one with a proscenium and real lights, not clamp lamps and fairy lights, which is extremely unlikely in my opinion, but if this were to happen, then the performer would have to imagine the people she's talking to. This would be most distressing, as it may offer an opportunity for acting, which I believe should be avoided at all costs.)

Did you have enough to eat?

How did you sleep? Hey, I'm sorry I got in bed with you—it was an accident! That used to be my bed. You kept right on dreaming. I'm glad.

Should we lock up? I'm not sure I have the key?

Should we leave a light on?

Did you go down to the water one last time? What did I leave behind? I always leave something behind. I just don't know what it's going to be this time.

I can't tell you how happy I am you all decided to come with me. But this is where we're going to have to split up. See, *you* are going to have to follow *me*. Relax! You can use the red car.

Maybe I should have made a map. Anybody mind getting lost?

I'll tell you what I can do. I can describe the import landmarks so that when we go by them, you'll know: we are on the right path.

We'll head out of town. North, about two miles. Out the Dixie Highway. And the first thing you'll notice, on your right, is a Denny's. Not just any Denny's! This is the very same Denny's where I used to have dinner with my mother on my father's golf nights.

(*She sees the Denny's floating somewhere just above the heads of the audience.*)

Oh, my God! THERE WE ARE!

Hunched over the menus, lost in the smell of fresh Formica, potato salad, and things, in general, frying, my mother straightens her bifocals. She folds up her menu.

"I want to ask you a question, young lady. Do you like boys or girls, or both?"

(*I am tempted to add the performer giggles nervously. But I think that that is obvious. Besides how many other ways are there to giggle? It's a serious question, and you may address your replies to the publisher of this tome.*)

I lean forward, my nipples grazing the shrimp in a basket.

"Both," I said. "I like both."

"Well, no wonder you can't hold down a full-time job," my mother says.

And the waitress overhears. She swoops down, apologizing, cocktail sauce in one hand, tartar sauce in the other.

"Oh, I'm so sorry! I should have guessed! I should have asked!
You can have both, honey. Here, help yourself!"

And then we'll pass by Apple Mountain.

It's not really a mountain. It's a pile of landfill they seeded over
with a few diseased elms. I know what you're thinking. You're thinking it's tacky to have a mountain made out of garbage. Well, you can
say that now. But you're new to Michigan. You live here as long as I
have, and you are going to crave any kind of mountain you can get
your hands on.

There's just a little too much *sky* out here.

There must have been some kind of remission. It was Septem-
ber, late. The light was something you could taste. He walked ahead.
His cane clobbering the goldenrod, the Queen Anne's lace. He picked
me up and put me on his horse.

I wasn't afraid! *I was two inches from the sun.*

I can still feel it. The slow curve of the earth. A dying man's
hands on my body. Seven hundred pounds of palomino between my
legs!

Dear God: let me feel it again.

Giddy-up! I moved. The horse moved. The whole world
moved.

Separately.

(*The performer approaches a member of the audience. It
helps if it's someone you could take a shine to. Someone
who might shine back at you. I always recommend
delivering the following at point-blank range.*)

Do you realize the entire solar system is moving?
Twelve miles a second towards the constellation Hercules?
Is that news to you?
I knew it the first time I kissed you.
Back then I laughed.
I asked my grandfather to take my shirt off.
I thought: *I will never fall.*
Are you hungry?

Excuse me, but I'm worried about you. You look like you could be hungry. Hey, if you're hungry, we'll just stop. I wouldn't mind.

I know a place we can go. A great place. The H and H Bakery. In Pinconning! I used to think it was named after me. So did my sister. But she didn't care for the place.

I stopped there with my sister, my mother, two friends of mine . . .

Where was my father?

My mother was being so nice to me I didn't recognize her. She let us sit in a booth! She let us order milk shakes! She even promised to take all of us girls to *Deer Acres*. Then, out of the woods, a porcupine started waddling across the parking lot.

"Look, girls! *A porkie!*"

My mother called porcupines "porkies." Skunks she called "wood pussies."

"You wait right here."

Mom ran out of the restaurant and dashed out to the Buick and popped open the trunk. And she lifted out an ax.

Porcupines have no *natural* enemies. No one wants a mouth of quills. Porcupines know this. They don't even know how to run. Unfortunately.

I don't know how many times she must have hit the damn thing. Long after it was dead. Maybe someone in the restaurant kept count. They were all looking.

Then my mother came back into the restaurant, her hands full of bloody flesh and quills.

"Girls! Something for your class! Science!"

It could have been worse. *It could have been a lot worse!*

She put down the ax.

If you look quick, you'll see the house I grew up in. The house she almost died in. The day the ambulance came it was really hot, but her hands were already ice. She was just lying there. Moaning. Little xs where the eyes should be. You know, like in a cartoon. Yeah, it was funny.

When the paramedics came into the room, she started fussing

with her bedclothes. She ran a blue hand through her hair. She opened her eyes and turned to the tallest one and asked:

"Are you going to check me out?"

I couldn't believe it! My mother was *flirting . . . on her death-bed!* I hadn't seen her that frisky in a year. The paramedics took her vital signs. Then they asked to see me in the hall.

Where was my father?

"Your mother's very sick."

"Yes. I know that. That's why she needs to go to a hospital."

"No, she doesn't. Not anymore."

I went back in the room. I bent over her. The last of the peonies lay face down, in the dirt. I could hear those men, out in the hall. I could smell them waiting. Wanting a cigarette.

"Holly," she asked. "Holly? Did you check out the tall guy? What a set of buns. I could almost taste them. I can't do anything about it, but you could."

The paramedics came back in the room. My mother turned to the tallest one and purred:

"Why don't you just pick me up?"

And he did. He did. That's how she went out of the house for the last time. In the arms of the ambulance man, talking dirty to him in her emphysemic wheeze. Her voice. It sounded like stale air forced through a bellows one last time. I was the fire she fanned.

Just for the record, he actually did have quite a nice set of buns. But that's another story.

(She leans back in the chair. She's home.)

Here we are!

This is my land. It used to be my mother's land . . . what am I saying? It still is my mother's land.

In this house, my mother refuses to sleep. She prefers to watch *me* sleep. In the eyes of my mother, I sleep the way a blind woman swims underwater. If she weren't still whispering in my ear, I don't think I'd ever wake up.

Wait here. I'll open the door.

> (*Blackout. She begins speaking into a microphone,
> whispering, and the lights slowly come up, excruciatingly
> slowly, to a very low level. A ghost light. Her manner is
> tender as though she were speaking to a very small and
> very frightened child.*)

Sssh. Listen to me. Listen to me.
Was that you crying?
Yes, it was. Don't lie to me.
Don't you think I'd know your cry by now?
In here, in the dark, alone. Like a baby.
Whose baby are you anyway, huh?

> (*She waits for a reply that doesn't come.*)

Look at me. I'm just like you.
I used to be a baby. I was scared.
Everybody's scared and nobody's scared enough. Ssssh.
There is something I've got to tell you.

I don't have any underwear on. Sssh! Don't cry.

> (*She settles back in the chair and sinks back into her
> world where everything happens in the past tense. When
> she begins to speak again, she's proud, triumphant, a
> former starlet on the verge of a comeback.*)

I sleep in the big bed all by myself. It's dangerous, oh, I know! On the other hand, I can really spread out. Take up all the space I want like . . . Africa! People see me, on the street, in the day, and they think: "What a small woman! Who would be afraid of her!"

But they haven't been to bed with me.

What do they know about fear?

At night, in bed, I'm a really big woman for my size.

I remember the first time I came to this bed, the first time I saw Africa, I had on a really good pair of boots. Talk about animals!

Back then, there were animals as far as the eye could see—right in this very bed. I wasn't afraid. I was hungry. I was very eager to get at least one pelt from every species.

It's not like now! These days, everything I touch, even this bed—it's all turning into . . . *Europe* . . . on me!

But this is my bed. This is my bed.

I said: "Let that man come to my bed with his guns out like that, let him take whatever he wants—there's plenty more. There's a lot more to me than he can kill. He's just a man. He used to be a . . . *baby!* He's afraid of me."

With good reason.

I am a continent.

Trees grow through me. Trees whose roots go all the way to the other side of the world, where they bloom as roses. Peace roses, tea roses. Roses named after all the dead presidents and their mistresses.

All these roses. Where do they come from? Right out of the top of my head. *I made them up.* So could you! We're both the same. We're both full of roses.

We need rain, don't we?
I don't remember why.
I am raining.
I am the rain.
I don't remember why.
I'm nobody's baby.

> (*She opens her eyes but doesn't look at anyone yet. She takes a long drink of green water from the vase. The lights slowly fade up to a brighter general wash. There is a sense of waking up, of coming to.*)

All I really wanted from my mother was her French.

> (*The woman leans back in the chair and closes her eyes. From offstage—left preferably—comes the sound of an*

accordion. I'd prefer a set of bagpipes, but an accordion is acceptable, considering the great shortage of accomplished lesbian bagpipe players. Not that I can tell the difference between well- and badly played bagpipes. To me both sound like my Welsh corgi did when she was hit by the car. The song should be sweet, like a tune you almost remember from childhood. Keep it upbeat, por favor. The woman smiles; the song is her reverie set to music.

Suddenly, her eyes open. She realizes the song is something she's remembering; it isn't merely a part of the dream. There is a mad accordionist—or bagpiper—loose on the premises. Sure enough, a woman enters playing aforementioned instrument. She is tall, broad shouldered, good bones, at once elegant and eccentric. Think of a Midwestern Marlene Dietrich. She's wearing a smoking jacket and very little else other than the instrument. Hopefully, she'll remind you of those Saturday mornings when your dad would dress up like Clark Gable and chase your mother around the breakfast nook with his semiannual hard-on. As the song progresses, the woman in the chair relaxes and lets herself sink back into the dream. When she starts speaking, it's as though she were dictating a letter into a foreign language, one she barely knows.)

I used to say . . . "Mama, I can't sleep at night. I smell the ocean! And I'm not talking about that far-off Atlantic or that unbelievable Pacific, oh, no. I'm talking about that old ocean. I'm talking about that blue blanket that used to cover this country. All of us. From the teenage anorexics to the Burger King evangelists.

"All of us. Sleeping with the dinosaurs, the black-capped chickadees, our heads—full of fish!

"That's the ocean that floods my bed each night, and what can I do about it?

"Mama?"

I get up in the morning. I get up in the morning, and the world—it's just so flat and dry. There's no hint, in the parking lot, in the mall, in the 7-Eleven, of why I am so full of ocean.

Do you know what I saw? I have to tell you what I saw.

I saw this boy grab a cat, sit on it—and pee all over it! I saw a man hit his wife so hard the whole house cried. I swear. The big blue colonial was weeping to see this woman, down on her hands and knees, picking up the three-bean salad. Picking it up, bean by bean.

All I want to do is sleep, Mama. I'm just like everyone else.

But I can't. I'm sinking, I'm turning to stone because of what I saw that night. That woman's blood and tears—right there! On the dining-room shag. Snaking out of her, spelling out curses in a language NOT English. She was saying: "*I'm sorry, I'm sorry,*" with her mouth. But her blood was singing another tune.

It was singing *sorrow, death.* Death to all of us in this woman's tears.

Am I the only one who can read tears?

I can't watch TV anymore. I just can't watch TV anymore. There's always some guy on TV, laughing. Everyone's laughing with him. Except for this woman. And me. I know she's gonna cry enough tears in the next week to flood us all out of our homes. Even the ones who are laughing.

Am I the only one who's afraid of drowning?

Teach me to *swim,* Mama. Teach me how to read this sorrow so I can resist the common current. Mama, teach me that French!

Mama says: "What makes you think I know any French?"

And her voice, it's just cool and blind—but! And this is a big "but"! She puts her hand on her hips, and I see her hips move under that wraparound skirt, so heavy and full, and I can smell the memory of ocean drifting out from between my mother's legs. Oh, there's real power in my mother's hips!

Let me tell you what I've seen. I've seen her hand, with its tapered fingers, run from her hips down to her thighs. I've seen her tongue sneak out of her mouth to wet her lips when everyone else was just watching TV. And I know, I know my mother is full *of French.*

The two of us? We're just two of a kind. She gets up when the rest of us sleep to do a slow and sultry striptease for her audience of prize African violets and oh! How they bloom!

And me? Well, the first thing you got to remember about me is I was born feet first. That's right. Feet first. After forty years of living inside her I came out, feet first, wearing this dress, high heels, and this bracelet.

I guess you could say I was *born* to speak French.

(*The woman's tone is important throughout this section, beginning with the strip in the bathroom. Her attitude should be one of an initiate witnessing a sacred ritual, a mystery revealed. The tone is one of awe, which could and probably will be misinterpreted as fear and will lead some to read this as incest. Give it your best shot, and hope for the best.*)

Mama took me to the bathroom and started asking me questions. Taking off her clothes and asking me questions. With every garment I got a new question.

She unbuttons her blouse and asks: "Do you want to know where babies come from?"

She shimmies out of her skirt and says: "Are you ready for the meaning of life? I mean the secret life. I'm talking about the French night club where we're all dancing. The hidden room where we stash our gold."

She says this, and VOILA!

My mother's got no underwear on!

Her pantyhose . . . it's down there, on the ground, sulking, feeling sorry for himself. Then that ole pantyhose just slinks on out of there, belly to the ground.

And my mother is standing in front of me . . . NAKED. Sssh! NAKED and glowing! Bigger than life. Shining from the inside out, just like that giant jumbo Rhode Island Red hen in front of the Chicken Palace and Riborama.

And she smells like salt, and she's promising me grease. Something to suck on, and she's asking me in. She's asking me in. And my legs are trembling, just like a diver's legs, because she's high above that sweet, pink ocean, that body of water that is a body, the body we call Mother, and I'm about to go in.

Mama says: "Holly, if something's bothering you, and you want to know the answer to it, just remember the answer is inside you." And with that she reached inside herself, and then she pulled her hand out. I could see how wet she was.

And the smell? Let me tell you about the smell. That smell made me want to do the mashed potato. I don't know why, but I just felt like dancing. Me and my naked mother dancing in the split-level.

She said she liked to smell herself. She said she liked to see herself open to nothing but her own eyes, because it made her a better gardener. It's as though her purple lips gave her a certain sympathy for the tomatoes. She could get them to go red when everybody else had a yard full of little mean, green fists of fruit.

She knew *she* was a tomato. Crawling through the mud. Or some species of rose that was forced to climb the sides of houses.

She said: "Holly, I know you're afraid of the world—and with good reason. You remember my father? He was a trout fisherman. And what did he use for bait? Mice, live mice. He'd chop off their legs and tie them to a hook. Oh, they were so *attractive* before they drowned. That's what fish like. And I started to beg for those fish—*that's what's scary!* I know you're afraid of the world and with good reason. But Holly, *this is your clitoris.* Let me tell you what she does for a living. It doesn't do any good to be afraid of the world!"

> (*The woman with the accordion quickly picks up the*
> *pace, and the alleged performer dances around the set.*
> *Something of a waltz persuasion perhaps, but the kind of*
> *waltz you'd want to do when you're done up in a dress*

from Frederick's of Hollywood. The performer speaks as
she flops back down in the chair.)

That's what we call using the space. Hey, it's performance art—it's
not supposed to make sense! You're lucky I'm using vowels tonight!

Years later I'm in school. I'm trying to learn everybody else's
French, and I'm saving my milk money. Working on a hunch that there
is going to be some kind of palomino in my future, when I discover a
big problem.

I'm telling the story I just told you to my best friend at that
time—Jodeen *Windy* Thompson—and all of sudden, she's looking at
me funny. Like I'm bleeding or something. Like seeing my mother's
pussy is some sort of *crime*.

But that's not the way I saw it. To me it was a gift. It was the
best thing she ever did for me. It was my inheritance.

Then Jodeen *Windy* Thompson said: "If it was so damn good,
how come you're crying?"

And I gotta say: "Jodeen *Windy* Thompson, you know damn
well I spent my entire childhood in church. Hoping to see Jesus! Did
I ever see him? No! Now I finally did! *I saw Jesus between my mother's
legs!* And when you see Jesus, you're gonna cry, too!"

Do you know what she said?

She said: "Holly, MY MOTHER does NOT have a PUSSY,
and if she did—*I would not want to know about it!*"

Am I surprised? No! It's no wonder she can't grow jack shit in
that tired old garden of hers! Her mother couldn't keep a cactus wet.
But you gotta feel sorry for them. They're just a couple of roses that
were forced to bloom underground.

What if the worst is true?

Do you ever think that? You're just going along, and all of a
sudden you ask yourself: "What if the worst is true?"

Do you know what that would mean?

That would mean that the feminists and the born-agains ARE
BOTH RIGHT. That would mean that seeing your mother's pussy IS
the birthplace of sin. That would make my mother nothing other than

a snake in housewife's clothing. And that apple she's offering me? A poison apple.

But do you know what?

I'd bite anyway. I'd bite again tonight if I could, and I don't care how many NEA grants it would cost me.

Because I would rather know what a snake knows than to grow up to be Jodeen *Windy* Thompson. You know, the kind of woman who's doomed to drown in her own body. Doomed to wear her body like it was somebody else's clothes. Doomed to die never realizing her mother had anything other than AstroTurf between her legs. Miniature golf! Hole in one!

Oh, the things they teach you in school.

I'm in school, and I discover Big Problem Number Two. You see, the French I got from my mother, and the French they're trying to teach me in school—*they don't match.*

They're trying to tell me that my mother didn't know French. They're trying to tell me her way of talking, with her tears and her pussy and with her sentences which could say "death" but mean "pleasure" in the same breath, and her words—her words which were like fifteen gold bracelets sliding down the arm of a woman dancing in a French nightclub—they're saying: "That's not French. That's not the *real* French."

In fact, they're saying that none of what was said between us was real at all.

Do you know what I learned in school?

I learned in school that there's no word, in French or in any language that I know, for the kind of woman my mother was. There's no word, in French or any other language that I know, for a woman who is a mother and a woman at the same time. There's no word, in French or any other language that I know, for a woman who had that kind of power over tomatoes! But, I swear, I saw it happen!

Maybe I made it up.

What about the time she's out of the house, and I'm there alone with my best friend at that time—Richard Goodsell. Now I like Richard—he's funny and he's smart—but he's a little too bony and nervous to have any other friends but me. His fingers are always bloody from sawing away at that damn violin, night and day! So, of course, Richard is getting the shit beat out of him—pardon my French—on a regular basis.

So I have to go to bed with him.

Don't get me wrong. I like Richard, but it's not like I want to do anything with his . . . thing. That would be so weird! It'd be like playing the violin in the bathtub . . . Richard does that. But still I like him. In that *animal* sort of way. They won't let the horses be alone in the barn. Not the best horses. So, this time, when Richard gets the shit beaten out of him—pardon my French—I get right on top of him. I get right on top of him, and I try to iron the tears out of that scrawny bag of bones.

Then my mother comes home.

She tries to pull me off of him. Yeah, she tries. But I fight just like a horse going out of a burning building, because sometimes, you don't know why, but you just got to go up in flames.

She's screaming: "What are you doing?"

And I'm screaming: "You don't understand!"

But I look at her. She's crying. I don't understand.

Because my mother is looking at me and crying, saying: "*I don't want you to be like me. I don't want them to do to you what they did to me!*"

Okay, Mom.

That was the time I stopped seeing my mother as a woman who had invented her own language, one where she was the engine inside every vowel she had. She stopped looking like a magician. She looked like a liar.

Do you know what they said about my mother?

They said: "Holly, your mother is crazy. Nobody did anything to her. She's just crazy."

And I started to agree.

A little while later, we were both right. My mother was one crazy bitch.

Shortly thereafter I went to art school!

(Music up; loud, dance music. French Bobby Darin dance music. The performer howls at the moon, real or imagined. The accordion player puts down her instrument, grabs a mike, and starts belting out her best faux French. The song is known as "Viva Lawn Chair" and consists of vaguely gallic noises punctuated with words like: "ratatouille," "Chevrolet," "Coupe de Ville," "Jacques Cousteau," and "Kalamazoo." The song is over when either the performer, singer, or audience is exhausted.)

I can't tell a lie.

I'm sorry! I guess if you came to see lies, you're out of luck.

I tried to learn how to lie in art school. Which is a really good place to learn how to lie. When I was there, I really tried to believe in certain art school lies. I tried to believe that *great art* was *universal*. I tried to believe that *great art* transcends the grubby, artless ghettos of gender, race, sexual preference; that *great art* is *abstract* and never gets blood on his clothes. Even witnessing a murder. Oh, no! Art turns the other way and looks out the cubist window. And even though I can *parlez-vous* with the best of them, even though I know how to lie by abstraction, allusion, inference, irony (the tools of modern art are at my disposal!), still, my mother's invented French is a lot stronger. It just keeps bleeding through all that art school training.

I just can't keep my mother's pussy out of my artwork.

It's as though seeing her cry that day cracked me open. Maybe that's why I can't shut out the deaths of Lisa Steinberg and the witch trial of her mother, the death of Jennifer Levin, and all those other deaths I feel inside.

But I don't have their names.

I don't have their names because the women were too dark or poor or queer or hot to get seen with the naked eye of journalism and forget about art.

I know ranting like this is going to ruin what's left of my art career. But I think I'm getting too crazy to be an artist any longer. Even in the East Village. I just can't tell a lie much longer.

On the bus going uptown the other day, two black men in work clothes were sitting across from me. One man says: "White people are killing me."

His friend says: "I know."

Then he says: "They hate us so much they don't even know they're doing it. They hate us, *but we're supposed to like them.* If you hate them, you're crazy."

His friend says: "I know."

Then the first man says: "They say they don't hate blacks, but look who they put in the White House! And I do mean the *White* House! And I'm supposed to like them."

His friend says: "I know."

"I hate them. I hate their women. I hate their children. Those stupid little white babies. Have you ever noticed how many white people are having babies these days?"

I can't tell a lie.

I always like it when someone who is black is nice to me. It helps me forget for a moment that I am a member of the DAR. My mother signed me up. She said: "I know how much you enjoy those women's organizations!"

When someone who is black is nice to me, I forget for a moment that I am descended from a long line of women who had elaborate gardens and plenty of domestic help. Women who, smiling, bent over each evening from a great height to feed the terriers and the black women big heaps of whatever it was their husbands wouldn't eat.

That's all in the past, right? Hey! I'm not racist, right?

I like dogs. I like the way dogs lick your hands. Helps me forget about all the species we've wiped out.

I can't tell a lie. I am hated, and I return the sentiment because it's just too big for art, and I'm getting too old for abstraction. I feel comfortable saying this because, after all, we're all women here tonight, aren't we?

Whoops. So we're not all women, but we're all lesbians! Any-one can be a lesbian! *Gender is no obstacle.*

Men just kill me. (*She is giggling and girlish throughout this section.*) They hate us women so deep and hard they don't even know they're doing it.

They say: "Hey, Holly, you're not talking about me. I like women. I even like you."

I'm very happy for you.

But what's this anti-abortion fever gripping the nation, huh? And what's this unending lack of funding for the children they suppos-edly cared so much about as fetuses and then abandoned as children?

I know what you're thinking.

You're thinking: "But there's *women* in the anti-abortion movement."

That's just what they want you to think. *But those are not women!* Nancy Reagan isn't even human. She's a hand puppet. Ever since with Kukla, Fran, and Ollie—no! And you never will.

What about some of my other favorite cocktail-party topics of conversation, like battered women. That's the way to really break the ice at a party—start talking about domestic violence! Really loos-ens everyone up.

You know what I read the other day in the paper? "If they don't like it, they could leave. Nicole Brown, Hedda Nussbaum—they could have just left."

But here's what I didn't read: *where are we supposed to go?* Show me on a map. My bags are packed; I'm ready to go. But please tell me: *where in the world can a woman walk?*

Yes, you're right! This is not art! Believe me, I've been told before. I wish I could be doing a little art right now. A little haiku, a little macramé. I'm just like everybody else. All I want to do is sleep.

I do know the difference between art and politics, even though it may not seem like I do. Remember—I went to art school. I didn't say I graduated, but I did matriculate. The first thing they said when they saw me coming through the door was: "Holly, please don't hit people over the head! Modern art is not supposed to hit people over the head!"

Fathers aren't supposed to hit daughters over the head either, and when Joel Steinberg hit his daughter, Lisa, so hard she died and when I read in the paper the next day, this columnist saying it was worse for her mother to not intervene than it was for her father to kill her, well, that was pretty much the end of this girl's macramé career.

Let me ask you a question.

Take all the time you want. It's something really bothering me lately. Why is it, if men don't hate women, like they say they don't, *why do they ask such stupid questions?* Why is it I'm always being asked: "Where are all the great women artists?"

You've got to be kidding. You don't know where they are?

They're out in the kitchen, making you a fucking cup of coffee, okay!

Let me ask you another question. Sort of in the same vein. Why is it, when I go to see a movie with my favorite movie star—Jodie Foster—in that movie she made a few years ago, *The Accused*, why was it that, during the rape scene *the men were cheering?!* I thought: "What is this? The Rose Bowl?" Why is it, when I went to see Almodovar's *Matador*, during the rape scene *the men were laughing?*

Do you really think this is *funny?* If you think this is funny, why don't you get your ass down to a rape crisis center and *man* a few hotlines, and YES, I do mean *man* the hotlines.

Okay. It's a bad idea. But hey! We could send the guys out for coffee! And they could clean the bathrooms. Don't worry—it's easy. You just got to make sure there's plenty of maxipads and odor eaters on hand.

Men are killing me! And they want me to like them. If you hate them, you're crazy.

(*Giggling, very teenybopperish.*) Well, I'm very sorry. But I don't. *I'm a man-hater!*

Of course, I don't hate men as much as a straight woman would but . . .

Hey, are you mad at me?

Are you gonna leave? That's okay. That's your right. This is a good time to leave. This is when most people leave. If nobody leaves,

I don't think I've done a very good job. If everybody leaves, I get to go home early.

What's the worst you have to say to me? What's it gonna be? *Whore?! Dyke?!* Nasty words. But actually I'm very happy. Because a woman only gets two choices: good girl and bad. So I got on the bad-girl bus because I thought it might be more fun. And let's remember that I'm a whore and a dyke for a very good reason.

I'm good at it.

Some people can sing, some people can dance, some people are double-jointed, and some of us just know how to fuck.

It's a gift. From God.

Do you have any idea how much I love you?

Do you think I'd waste my breath on you if you didn't break my heart? Look at me. I know you're afraid. Think how I feel. I know you're afraid, because I used to be a baby and I was afraid. Everybody's scared and nobody's scared enough.

But we did share a bed together. You remember that, don't you? Remember our bed, and answer me, why was, if you love me, if you love women, why was it that after the rape, you kept showing me picture after picture of black men, when I told you once—a thousand times—it was a white man who raped me?

What did you say? "*It could have been worse.*"

Why was it, after the rape, you said: "Holly, you're lucky he came. If they don't come, they like to kill"?

Is that so? Don't you know I slept with fifty men by the time I was twenty, and I never came with one of them, *but I never thought about killing them!*

Until tonight! Hey, it's never to late to set a new policy. I could make a little sign and hang it over the bed: "Get it right the first time, or pay the big price!"

Oh, listen, I know men are in pain. Their pain is *famous*. Their pain is going to be the death of me. Saying they love me. Saying they love women. I wish I believed them. But I don't. I think what they mean is: *boys will be boys.*

Thank you very much, but I'd rather be crazy.

About my words—when I say, "I hate men," you have to understand that hate is the dark side of love. But I'm not counting on you loving me back. I'm not sure you can hear what I'm saying.

I might as well be talking my private French.

Well, I was probably crying. And a man came up to me. Big guy, he looked familiar. He asked me what he could do. When he told me his name, I said, "Oh, well, you knew my mother when she was young. What was she like?"

He said: "I liked your mother. All the men in Saginaw liked your mother."

"She was pretty . . ."

"She was pretty all right. She was PRETTY unusual for a woman from Saginaw. There used to be a word for the kind of woman your mother was, and it started with an *s*."

"Are you trying to tell me that my mother liked to . . . um, dance?"

"Your mother liked to dance. She was a *shameless* dancer. And she knew *how* to dance."

I looked at this guy. I thought I should just spit in his face. I couldn't see his face very well because it was covered over by this enormous shadow cast by his oversize toupee. I probably should have just spit anyway. I mean, *it was her funeral*. But something stopped me. I believed him when he said that he liked her. He didn't mean to say anything bad about her.

After my mother died, seven blue herons flew right over the top of the Holiday Inn and landed smack dab in the middle of our front lawn, meaning . . . you tell me.

But after my mother died, I was having this dream about my mother and she was drowning. I went in the water after her, and she just kept swimming out farther, laughing, saying it was really silly for *me* to try to save *her* because I was the one who was drowning.

After my mother died, I probably don't need to tell you this, but all of my sentences started with "after my mother died . . . "

And then, a little while after my mother died, the only thing I really wanted to do was fuck.

So there's this guy, at work, right?

Always hovering over my PC. Asking me if I want to go to the Blarney Stone. So finally I got to say to him: "Look, buddy, *I hate you.* You're an idiot, and I'm a lesbian, and you touch, you're a dead man, okay?"

And he's laughing. I've never been so funny in my life.

After my mother died, I told him that she had died, and *he started to cry.* I couldn't believe it. This guy I thought was an idiot was crying, all over the copier about my mother. And I thought: "Okay maybe you're gonna get lucky after all."

All of a sudden, I knew what I wanted. I wanted to be nasty.

I wanted to be nasty in Spanish. If you're gonna do it, you might as well do it in Spanish. It sounds a lot better: *sin vergüenza.* I wanted to be *desnuda* in my terrarium with this junior account executive from Middle Village, Queens. I wanted to be outside of history, I wanted to rewrite the Bible. So I said: "Let's go to the Blarney Stone." We went, and we knocked back a few pink squirrels.

Then I took him downtown.

On the Lexington Avenue local, he detailed the various disgusting acts he would commit to my defenseless body, and then he asked me what I had in store for him.

I said: "Okay, cowboy. Here's the program. You're on the menu. We're gonna take the plunge. We're gonna go for broke. I got plans to rewrite the Bible tonight, and when I get through with you, this is the way it's gonna read from now on: 'Oh, they were naked at last! *Cara a cara entre azul y buenas noches.* Face-to-face between blue and holy nights. Two ficus trees. Two alley cats. Two ancient jade plants growing out of the same straw hat. You could just call this a walk-up Garden of Eden. And the first words spoken were: *Ooh-la-la.*'"

I will translate. This means they were naked and they knew it and *they didn't care!* They didn't care about the white trash across the air shaft and they didn't care about the Ukrainian ladies across Saint Mark's Place with their raw elbows propping up opera glasses and they didn't care about the Blue Oyster Cult fans that lived downstairs from them. Who couldn't see them but might be able to hear the second words spoken, which were: *Ooh-la-la.*

Adam begging Eve to sit on his face. Well! By now Eve's fingers are just a galloping up and down Adam's fly, and our heroine decided to treat Mr. Adam to a little seminar. So she reaches out and grabs him, Italian style, and says:

"Mr. Adam, *querido* señor! God has sure lied to you. You're not the first man. You're just *the first man this month*, ooh-la-la! That sound of zippers? That's *holy*. You can hear the word of God in it. Jesus does love us, even though he hasn't been invented yet. Jesus loves you, Mr. Adam, and those luscious polycotton Sansabelt pants, because Jesus loves that getting-naked sound almost as much as you love my tits.

"Yes, I know they're perfect. *They came in the mail.* Just last month from the Fruit of the Month Club. Or it could be that they didn't exist at all until you started sucking on them . . .

"Mr. Adam! What is the meaning of that . . . edifice . . . I see leaning out of your pants like that? I haven't seen anything so *interesting* since my last trip to the Vatican.

"And Mr. Adam: *Aquí está la pregunta du jour*:

"Where you want to do the monkey business? Anything is possible as long as you remember this:

"*We are the sons and daughters of meat.*

"*We are barely descended from mud.*

"This is the start of history. Starting with my hand, wet, on your wet dick. *Which is wetter, Adam or Eve? Which is closer to the sea?*"

Adam says: "I don't know, baby. Let's just do it against the wall."

And he presses her against the wall, and then he spreads her legs like a . . . I don't know. Like nothing else could, because, *recuerda*, this is the beginning. Beginning with Mr. Adam sliding in his cock kind of slow, kind of very slow, a little too slow for this heroine. But what the hell—this is a work of *fiction*!

This is also quite an unusual section of the narrative. In fact, in my entire oeuvre. In fact, you might be wondering why I've claimed I've been a victim of homophobia at all. But when the federal government sent agents to inspect my art . . . you may not realize that the federal government inspects art and beef in much the same way. In fact, I think they're the same people! Poking and prodding and check-ing for fat content—the higher the better!

I told the federal art inspectors they had to view this piece, particularly this section, in the light of my overall artistic goals. I told them about my ten-point plan to advance lesbianism globally, using song, dance, and monologue.

This is only step one.

I think of it as E-Z Listening Lesbianism. Or Lesbianism 101. And remember, in the eyes of Jesse Helms, all the blow jobs in the world just won't erase one muff diving.

It's not the kind of hairs he likes to split.

This is also the part in the narrative where I admit: *maybe I was wrong*. Maybe I've been a little harsh on Mr. Adam. He's no dumbo. He knows that shame didn't just ram its way into the newborn human mind. Oh no. *Tragedy takes time*. More time and care than the sixteen thrusts average for average heterosexual coitus. According to condom research.

Just one of those things I know.

Adam is happy. Eve is happy. They're both happy there's Sheetrock surrounding this Garden of Eden. And then Mr. Adam is very happy because he is all the way inside her, and he can feel her feel him hit—paydirt.

All of a sudden, Eve has got to say: "Yo, buddy! Do you know who I am? Do you have any idea at all who you are porking? I'm the preeminent lesbian performance artist from southern Michigan!"

All Adam says is: "Hot damn, baby. All I knew about you is how wet you were." And he gives it to her a little bit harder and asks her if she has any hobbies.

Eve doesn't say anything about her hobbies. Eve doesn't say nada about nada, because, praise the Lord, *words fail her*. She can see her mother—dancing!—*in Dayton*! She can see herself on the outside of history where *todo el mundo se habla español*.

I'm going to translate.

That means where everyone is shirtless, shameless, good for nothing but being bad.

Sin vergüenza.

When you think of me, eat an apple.

Chew very carefully. I'm still your apple. Lick every bit of juice that drips down your chin and say: "Help me. I want to change. Let me be changed."

It could happen. Didn't it happen at least once? Didn't it happen that night I held you, and I ate you until your singing golden skin was all the way inside me? Weren't you changed then? Weren't you an apple then?

It's not always February. We don't always drink this weak tea.

Even for my father and my mother there was a late August. When she got sick, he took very good care of her. He could understand her at last. She was just like work to him.

See my mother on the last night of her life?

My father bends over the scrawny bed. I could see the bones in his face for the first time. He feels like a farmer towards her.

"Help me," she says.

And he does. He kisses her. Not gently. Her mouth is open, and I can see his tongue.

Apples are suddenly everywhere.

The fly is out of the amber. The teapot boils down in the western sky.

Help me. I'm dying to change.

She pulls him on top of her. Her hands go between her legs. On the last night of my mother's life, my father's hand is red. Red? Red from the light of apples falling. Suddenly apples fall like rain outside their bedroom window.

I get it: *after she's gone, we'll still have pie.*

And now I see my mother touch my father. I see him shimmy. I see him change. I see him, yes, I can see him.

He is an apple. In her hands.

THE END

Clit Notes

This is one of my girlfriend's favorite jokes: A drunk goes to the opera. Soon after the curtain goes up, he starts bellowing: "Sing 'Melancholy Baby'!" The performers ignore him, and the show goes on. But he keeps demanding: "Sing 'Melancholy Baby.'" Finally, it's time for the diva's aria, and the drunk stands up in his seat to bellow: "If you can't sing 'Melancholy Baby,' at least show us your cunt."

I used to begin the classes I give on developing autobiographical material for performance by asking everybody to tell me why they're there. But I've discovered that beginning with this joke gives me a much better sense of the lay of the land. First of all, it helps me identify the students who will soon come to see themselves as the members of the opera company bravely struggling to preserve the traditions of high culture in spite of inebriated philistines like myself. Most of the students will grin slightly and wonder if they've missed the punch line, which gives me a perfect opportunity to explain what the joke is.

First of all, it isn't the world's greatest joke. But it is a good way to answer the perennial question: what is performance art? All of the basic food groups of performance art are in this story: pop culture, high art, spectacle, big hair, substance abuse, and pussy—it's all in there! I tell the class that in order to appreciate performance art you've got to imagine yourself sitting in the audience far enough back so that what's happening in the audience and what's going on onstage are all part of the show.

It was in this spirit that I decided to call this piece *Clit Notes*. Many of my staunchest fans saw the title as the equivalent of the drunk's demands to see the singer's cunt. One friend said the title had nothing to do with what the show was about, and if I was going to insist on *Clit Notes*, I should include either more clit or more notes to justify the title. She claimed the only reason I gave it that name was I wanted to force people to say "clit."

Which was, of course, totally true. But after all I see myself as a political artist, and I think that making more people wrap their mouths around the word, if not the thing itself, is precisely the kind of political goal one can hope to realize through theater. Why is it that the words *dick*, *prick*, and *cock* seem to pop up everywhere I look? I've been told that the reason is that *dick* is also a proper name, that *prick* is also a verb, the sun also rises, and the poppy is also a flower but that—and I quote!—"the clit is just a clit."

Please! Not in my experience! If they had said: "The clit is a clit," I might agree—it sounds like what Gertrude Stein was trying to get at. But "just" a clit as in "merely a clit." No, I don't think so.

Before presenting this work I had no idea how far some people would go to avoid having to say this word. The *New York Times*, for example, wouldn't print the title, which was described as containing "a slang term for the word 'clitoris.'" Before going on the air on some National Public Radio station, I was told I could use the word only if I was talking about myself. Under no circumstances, I was warned, could I call someone else a clitoris on the air.

Of course, it's hard to work under these conditions. But somehow I managed, with the help of Dan Hurlin, whose role in this production might be described as more than a director but less than a dessert topping. This piece was commissioned by the New York Shakespeare Festival and developed with the help of Dixon Place and the New York Theater Workshop. I'm also indebted to the feedback I got from Nina Mankin, Eleanor Savage, Tim Miller, David Cale, David Roman, and especially Phranc.

****

*Centerstage, a ten foot square of diagonal yellow and
black stripes. In the middle there is a small wooden*

school chair. The performer who does not see herself
as middle-aged enters and stands behind the chair. She
is wearing a red dress. (Under no circumstances
should this piece be attempted in anything other
than a red dress!)

The first time I was in love with another woman?

Actually, *she* was a *woman;* I was just thirteen. In fact, this little anecdote might have a happier ending if there'd been some sort of gay youth organization in my hometown. Some sort of North American Woman-Girl Love Association. But, nooooo!

The men, they get everything good.

The lesbian chicken, who worries about them, huh?

(She sits down in the chair.)

Her name—and this was an important part of the attraction— her name was *A—Neee—Ta Weeen—dttt.* Which I discovered sounded an awful lot like "I needa whip," if you said it enough times to yourself.

And I did.

She was a social studies teacher. That's what we called history in my hometown of Saginaw, Michigan. I know I don't have to tell you that Saginaw, Michigan, is the Navy Bean Capital. Of the *world.* You may have also heard of it in that Simon and Garfunkel song: "It took us four days to hitchhike from Saginaw." They had connections, of course.

But what they taught us was not actually history. There's laws against teaching history in Michigan. What they taught, instead, was amnesia. So, by the time I was thirteen, all I knew about World War Two, for instance, was what I had gleaned from *Hogan's Heroes.* Funny little war!

I knew there were slaves at one time in America—and the Republicans freed them!

There were forbidden books in my hometown. In fact, most books were forbidden. They were on the library shelves, but you had to get a note from home to read them. I was not about to get a note from my home to read a book. My mother used to drop my sister and me off after school at Republican headquarters so we could stuff envelopes for Nixon. Even when he wasn't running. No one wanted to break the news to us. "Keep hope *alive*." It was my mother's idea of day care.

Anita Wendt used to slip me these forbidden tomes. Books like: *The Autobiography of Malcolm X, I'm O.K, You're O.K.*, and *Jonathan Livingston Seagull.*

For some reason this made me love her.

I guess I loved her because she was the one who woke me up.

This love had an unfortunate way of expressing itself in the eighth grade. Sometimes I'd be in class, and I'd think: "Her mouth! It's a *magnet*. I am going to kiss her, *and there's nothing anybody can do to stop me!*"

So I just throw myself to the ground and writhe around, hoping people would think I was merely epileptic. A little foaming at the mouth is better than having people think you're *queer*.

And sometimes I'd be so inspired by her lectures that I'd go into a trance and start removing articles of clothing. Once I took my panty hose off in class. I have no memory of taking them off. But there they were! Down on the floor in an incriminating taupe heap.

I began to think there was something the matter with me, and if I weren't careful, I might start voting Democratic. I turned to the definite sexual authority of that and perhaps all time, Dr. David Reuben's *Everything You Always Wanted to Know about Sex.*

Just the table of contents was a real eye opener.

I noticed, right off the bat, that male homosexuals had their own chapter. But the females were just a footnote under "Prostitution."

Oddly, there was no separate heading for "Democrat."

So I read the whole damn thing. Up to this time, I thought homosexuality had to do with attraction between two people of the same sex. But not according to David Reuben. According to Dr. Reuben, the most unique feature of the homosexual, male or female, is their compulsive erotic relationship to household appliances.

And all that distinguishes the male from the female is that male homosexuals are forever shoving various appliances up their butt: Shot glasses. Blenders. Toaster ovens.

While on the other hand, the women are always strapping these appliances on: Electric toothbrushes. Color TVs. Washer-dryers. Ladies, start your engines!

I was thirteen years old, and it seemed to be a very shallow and materialistic form of love. And I realized that being a homosexual—if you were going to be any good at it—would require an awful lot of leisure time. Not to mention electrical outlets.

And it was somewhat rough on the environment.

But I read on.

Dr. Reuben said that, like cancer, impending lesbianism had its warning signals. The most ominous of which was, and I quote, "the enlarged clitoris of The Lesbian which can be inserted into The Vagina of her partner achieving a reasonable facsimile of The Real Thing."

Whatever that is.

Still I read on. Dr. Reuben said that "the most prized lesbians . . . " And I thought—*wait a minute!*

I had no idea there would be prizes! Hot dog!

Here I was, in the Midwest, county-fair country, and all of a sudden I could see the next Saginaw County Fair! There was the lesbian barn! Why, it was right next door to the Clydesdales! Down from the holsteins! All those people out on the midway saying: "Come on down at four; they'll be judging the lesbians. You don't want to miss that!" And all those little Four-H kids! Leading around all those lesbians they'd hand raised. Suckled from baby butch all the way up to full-blown bull daggers!

Dr. Reuben didn't mention what sort of prizes one might hope to win for being a lesbian. But I figured a few surge protectors might come in handy. I read on.

Dr. Reuben said that some of the blue-ribbon specimens had clits four! five! even six inches . . . long, I guess. He didn't say.

I think you know what I did.

I went to my father's workroom. I got his tape measure. It was twenty-five feet long. I figured: "That ought to do it!" You got to believe in yourself.

And I borrowed my mother's hand mirror. I went to my bedroom, dropped my skirt, and I ran into all sorts of problems. I could not find anything between my legs that looked like it could be inserted into the body of another person, even under the best of circumstances.

At this point I began to doubt the very existence of my clitoris.

It didn't seem like something someone in my family would have. Not after all that work for Nixon.

It didn't seem like something anyone in Saginaw would have. Or . . . maybe they used to have them, but Simon and Garfunkel took them with them when they left! I measured everything between my navel and my knees, and took the best score. Nothing was even four inches long.

Right then I knew I would never win any prizes for being a lesbian. I might not even be a dyke after all.

I didn't measure up.

(FADE TO BLACK.)

> *When the lights come up, the performer is sitting in a
> kitchen chair on the upstage right corner of the square. I
> recommend one of those vinyl and chrome kitchen
> chairs. The chair should remind the audience of egg-
> salad sandwiches and pickle spears.*

Soon as they opened my father up, they knew. Probably knew before.

Malignant.

At first I thought: "Big deal. You have two kidneys. You lose one, it won't kill you. Plenty of people do fine on just one. Just because you lose a kidney, that's no reason to think you can't have a normal life."

If you go for that sort of thing.

Funny but this was exactly the same thought my father had

when he first found out that I was a lesbian. He didn't say anything. Silence had always been his first language. But by then I was fairly fluent. I knew what he was thinking. I knew he figured he had two daughters. So he lost one. Big deal. It wouldn't kill him. Plenty of people do fine on just one. One was more than enough for his purposes. Just because he had one daughter who was a dyke, no reason to think he couldn't have a normal life.

That's all he ever really wanted. A *normal life*. He got pretty close. He almost had a normal life.

Do you have any idea how many different kinds of cancer there are?

Jesus! It's like all the breeds of dogs. Each with their own habits. Temperament. Preferred hiding places. Each with their own special name. The name, that's important. Because the name is the key to the future. As in, whether there's going to be a future or not.

Of course, all of them will bite. But there's a difference in how hard. There's a difference in whether they'll let you go once they've got a hold of you.

It took two weeks for the doctors to give my father's cancer a name. To tell us what disease we were dealing with. I say "we" because, when sickness enters one person's body, it doesn't just stay there. It comes to live with everyone who loves that body, its appearance determined by the kind of love you have for the body where the sickness makes its home . . .

Fuck! I didn't just say I loved my father, did I?

I meant to imply I loved his *body*.

Which is not *him*. My *father*, his *body* . . . two completely separate entities. Barely on speaking terms.

Every night we waited for my father's diagnosis, his disease would rise out of his bed and come to mine. Every night of those two weeks his disease would lie on top of me, sucking my dreams dry till I just had one dream left.

I saw a vision of the last decade in this country.
I saw a landscape of death.

A country ruled by doctors, lawyers.
This was a vision that appeared to me in white, on white.

And when I say "white," let's be clear what white I'm talking about.
I'm talking about the white of the police-chalk line and especially the
white of the sheet pulled over the face when all you see of the eyes are
the whites.

I don't know about you but there's too many of my friends back
there. Too many people who belong to me only in the past tense. So
many that I start to think: "That's where I belong." At least that part
of me that could say, without any hesitation:

"I want to live. In my body. In the present tense.
In front of all these people
I'm going to tell the truth."

Not the whole truth. Not nothing but the truth. Not that one. Just
my little chunk of it. Without apology. I used to say: "I don't care who
hates me."

Who did I think I was?

It's like I thought I was playing some sort of game of tag, and
I was so sure that I was faster, smaller than that sweaty, balding guy
we've all decided was "it." Now that part of me is somebody else I lost.
Another face who appears nightly, asking to be remembered or at least
counted. Promising me, if I count all the dead, I'll sleep as deep as I
dare.

But there's too many of the dead to count.

So I won't sleep. What do I need with sleep anyway. Who can
sleep at a time like this, huh? Besides. Getting to sleep has never been
my biggest problem. My big problem is waking up.

I spent my entire childhood in a coma.

Then I turned twenty, and I kissed a woman. Sort of by accident. But she kissed me back. With a purpose. An intention I couldn't
guess. Something started happening to me. Something that the ex-

pression "coming out" doesn't quite cover. In my case, it was more a question of . . . coming to.

But the world is round.

And I resent that fact!

Soon as my father said he was sick, after my father said the word "cancer," I knew I had to go home. Going home does not come naturally to me. If my father's medium was silence, mine has tended to be escape. But there's no future in escape because the world is round. So the faster you run away, the faster you end up, right back where you started, face-to-face with whatever you were running away from in the first place.

Your worst fears, they're always the most patient.

Part of my reluctance in going home, no doubt, has to do with what my parents' home is. From the outside it looks oppressively normal. Your average, Middle-American, middle-class, middle-everything split-level.

But that's just the outside!

In reality, this is the entrance to a cave . . . cave . . . cave . . . cave . . . I know if I don't make myself as small as possible, if I'm not willing to pretend I don't even have a body, they'll never let me in the front door.

And as soon as I'm inside, I'll lose my footing. The floors are always slick with a mixture of prehistoric tears, come, light ranch dressing.

An outside light means nothing in this kind of darkness. Before I go home, I tie a rope around my waist and give the end to my friends:

"Don't let go of me. Don't let me fall. If I'm not back in two weeks, come after me, okay?"

I tell everybody I'm going back because of my father. But the truth is I'm going back because there's parts of my body I can't feel. Parts of me still dreaming, back in my father's bed. Waiting for some kind of wake-up call. A sign. A word . . .

Okay. I'll say it.

A kiss.

Something I'm never going to get from my father. Now that he's living with one foot in the grave and the other on a banana peel, as he would say, isn't it time for me to wake all the way up. Once and for all. Isn't it about time to get completely out of my parents' bed?

For two weeks I practice going home. Trying to get it right. I get up. In the middle of the night. Crawl to the mirror. And I can already see the toll my father's illness is taking.

I look just like the place I was born.
I'm a dead ringer for Michigan!
Can you see it?
I'm almost an island.
There's water on three sides of me.
A place carved up by ice.
The birthplace of all storms.
A short growing season.
All the cities shut down, the people moved to Texas.

I don't mean to brag. These could be my best qualities.

Step two. I try to get the woman in the mirror, the one who looks like Michigan, to repeat after me: "I want to live." A pep talk, but something goes wrong. The words swerve out of control and turn into questions. So it comes out like this:

"I want to live?
In my body?
In the present tense?
I want to tell the truth?
Which one? Mine? My father's?
Is that what I want to do with my life?"

Two weeks go by in this way. In the daylight I conduct a futile search for the doctor who said he could get me discount Prozac if I got him season tickets to WOW. Finally my father calls:

"I just want you to know. I have the good kind of cancer."

His voice is so thin. Already. It's like the skin on the under-side of arms where you can look and see—what do you know—the blood is still moving. Here's evidence that the heart's red oompah-pah band plays on. But it's still my father's voice. And he's talking to me in a tone I recognize, I remember. It's the one he used when I got to that age where everywhere I looked I saw snakes.

It got so bad I wouldn't go out of the house. But my father wanted me out in the world. He had done everything he could to make the world safe for me.

So he told me that there were two kinds of snakes. The good and the bad. What made the good ones good is that they ate things that were worse than any snake.

Gee, thanks, Dad. Now I had something new to worry about!

But my father assured me the snakes had everything under con-trol. A very hardworking species, apparently. So when I saw the grass move, when I saw the darkness under the trees roll itself into the let-ter S, what I was seeing was a friend. Just doing his job. Keeping me safe.

"And the bad snakes, Dad? What about them?"

I had to know! He said there weren't any. Not anymore. Not in the woods we called ours. My father insisted I was safe. Nothing with teeth big enough to bite us, not in our woods. If I heard some-thing howling at night, it was the wind. It couldn't possibly be a wolf. A coyote. Or a wolverine, ha! And the few neighbors looked just like us.

Still my father ran a thin wire around our eighty acres. Our woods. I remember him hanging up the big signs saying No Trespass-ing. I remember because I walked behind him. In his footsteps. Never asking what was the purpose of this fence. Who was supposed to be kept out. Who was being kept in. I couldn't imagine there was any-thing for the good snakes to eat. Who was lower than a snake? Just as I couldn't imagine that there was ever a time when these woods weren't ours.

I wanted to live.
In my body.
In our world.
All I wanted to be was my father's daughter.

I loved him because of his tools. His shotgun. His poison. The big sign
he made, black letters on white wood: Private Property. Keep Out.
Out of the corner of my eyes, I studied his hands. Massive. Like paws.
The big hands of a hard worker. He was always working, so I could
walk barefoot under the pines. Through our woods.

That my father has the good cancer doesn't mean he's going to
live. It means there is a drug. A treatment that might, as the doctors
like to say, buy him time. They like to say that, don't they, the doctors.
Because they're doing the selling and not the buying of this time.

Sure, you can live without a kidney. But how long do you last
without your bones, liver, lungs. Your brain. I mention these places
because these are the most likely places where, even as I speak, my
father's cancer is waiting, coiled out of the doctors' sight, waiting to
strike again.

And so I imagine it gliding through my father's body. Starting
down deep. Near the place where I used to live inside him. Moving
up and swallowing what's worse than cancer. What's already hurt him
more than dying ever could. Like being born in Appalachia. February
3, 1916. A family of coal miners. If they were lucky. My father and his
brother Wolf grew up in the orphanage. Not because there's no family. Because there's no money. When they get out, their mother dies
and still there's no money. When he's twenty-five, he's the last of his
kind. But now there's a little money. So he goes to a dentist for the
first time. And on that first visit, they pull all his teeth.

I'm probably being dramatic. They must have left one or two.
But I'm sure the cancer will get those, too.

And if this is what the doctors have promised, if this is really
the *good* cancer at last, then it's bound to eat most of my father's marriage to my mother. Their terrible fights. The silences which were worse.

Until the cancer gets to the worst thing of all.

Until it gets to that thing that my father says is what's really killing him. Anybody want to take a guess what is the worst thing that ever happened to my father?

You're looking at her.

(*The perfromer takes a little bow or curtsies.*)

Fall of 1990.

We haven't spoken in several months. I'm the one to pick up the phone. At the sound of my voice, he starts to cry. Weeping. Like there's been another death in the family.

"Why are you doing this to us?"

I try to tell him I'm not doing anything. I try to tell him something's been done to me.

"Don't give me that. I watch TV. I read the paper!
You're all over the place!
This is what you wanted! You always wanted to hurt us.
You're doing a good job.
My own daughter. Act like you had no shame. No family."

I wish I had no shame. Sometimes I think that shame is all I've got. It was a synonym in our house for "family." It was the crazy glue that kept us together, and I emphasize the word *crazy*.

I try to tell my father that the person he's seeing everywhere isn't me. It's somebody's idea of me. I've become a symbol. I've been buried alive under meanings other people have attached to me. I tell him that some of what he's heard are lies.

"So you're not a lesbian?
Is that a lie?
You don't stand in front of a lot of people and talk about having sex— with women—and you call that 'art,' and then you expect the federal government to pay for it.

You never did that?
That's a lie?
That's good news."

It's my turn to be silent, but my father isn't finished.

"Could you at least stay away from that goddamn Karen Finley?
Is that too much to ask?
Homosexuality, well, that's one thing.
But people who play with their food!
What did we ever do to you?
Just look at yourself.
You're never going to have a normal life, I hope you know that.
What was it? What happened to you? What went wrong?"

I take my father's questions seriously. I promise I will tell him what made me abandon any hope of ever having A Normal Life. I'll tell him. At least, as much as I remember.

Fade to black. When the lights come up, the school chair from the first section should be slightly downstage right of the square's center. The performer is pacing back and forth in front of the chair. She is speaking as though she were a distinguished professor giving a lecture at the Famous Performance Artist Correspondence School.

Performance Art: What Causes It?
Where it comes from and what can be done about it.
Three case studies.

Number One: "Performance Art as a Tool of Social Change."

(As the performer sits down, she slips into a softer, older self.)

I launched my careers as a lesbian and as a waitress simultaneously. For a while they kind of fed off each other; there was a certain symbiosis.

Someone has suggested this had something to do with me working in seafood restaurants, but you'd never catch me saying something so repulsive!

Initially, I admit I wasn't very adept at being either a waitress or a lesbian, although I was fast and mean, and this was a plus in both departments. I remember standing over the naked form of the woman I lived with. The woman who everyone in town thought was my girlfriend. Everyone, that is, but her. I wanted desperately to have my way with her. But I had no idea what my way might be.

Meanwhile, back at the Red Lobster, I was working very hard to present myself as a lesbian separatist waitress . . .

THAT'S NOT FUNNY!

It's not so easy to combine those particular sets of identities. If you want tips. It was hard to persuade anyone I was even the most benign form of feminist, since most of the women would run when they saw me coming. They knew I was apt to start quoting Ms. magazine at the slightest provocation, and that I loved to chase people around the salad bar trying to persuade them how oppressed they were.

But I was respected, if not actually liked, for the principled stances I would assume at our staff meetings, which were held every Tuesday at eight A.M.

The rest of the waitresses would just be trying to wake up. They'd be all hunched over a cup of our famous burnt coffee that we'd whiten with a little liquid paper we'd try to masquerade as cream. Eight A.M., and your feet are already rebelling against the vinyl prisons they've been sentenced to. And the manager, he's introducing the Bermuda Triangle Platter, or talking about the latest all-you-can-eat deep-fried sea monkey special. Or the drink du jour. The Moon Rocket. It was always our drink du jour no matter what jour it was, because it was blue and frozen and on fire. All at the same time.

And I'd say: "WAIT JUST A MINUTE!

While we're sitting here trying to come up with a few more ways to push shrimp cocktail, women in Africa are having their clitorises cut off! And I want to know: WHEN IS THE RED LOBSTER GOING TO DO SOMETHING ABOUT THAT!"

As a lesbian separatist, I was more successful as a separatist than I was as a lesbian. I pretty much separated myself from just about everyone.

It's something you never read about in radical political theory: *the loneliness of the pure.*

And I wanted so desperately to experience some of that sister-hood I had read so much about. Finally an opportunity presented itself in the form of a five-state employee talent contest.

My talent was choreography. It's only to the untrained eye that I appear to be sitting almost motionless in a chair. I decided to inflict my talent on all the waitresses because I had read: "None of us are free unless ALL of us are free!"

So I called all the waitresses together, and I put pillowcases over their heads.

Then I proceeded to interpret, choreographically, the wit and wisdom of my then heroine, Andrea Dworkin, as set to the music of Randy Newman's "Short People Got No Reason to Live."

This was my big chance! This was my opportunity to strike a blow against the capitalist patriarchy!

What do I look like—someone who's got all the answers?

So I told a joke instead.

And we won.

(*She becomes the professor again.*)

Number Two: "Breaking the Fourth Wall."

(*Back in the chair the performer changes, this time into the sullen, overprivileged brat she once was.*)

Like most children I had various chores I was expected to do around the house. The most odious of which was, in my opinion, kissing my parents good-night. I realized, however, it was an important job. One that apparently they could not do for themselves. And I would be paid.

One night, sitting next to my mother on the couch, I had a sudden epiphany. Fortunately, the fabric was Scotchgarded, so I didn't cause any permanent damage.

But all of a sudden I realized that my mother wasn't just my mother . . .

She was a *woman*.

I knew what that meant.

I'd already figured out that being female was a chronic medical condition. You couldn't cure it, but you might be able to learn to live with it. If you got the right treatment in time. And I had an idea for a new treatment for women.

I noticed I had an audience. This made me very happy because I'd heard in science class that a tree falling in the wilderness made no sound. I wanted the world to know about my new treatment for women. So I stood up and looked at my audience. It consisted of two people. My father and the other person who I will alternately refer to as my sister and my father's girlfriend.

It's important to know who your audience is.

I went over to my mother, and when I got to her, I straddled her. Kind of like I imagined I would straddle that pony I knew by then my father was never going to buy me. And as I mounted Mom, I turned, and I looked at my audience, as if to say: "I bet you wish you'd just bought that pony for me, now don't you? Maybe all this ugliness could have been avoided."

Then I proceeded to kiss my mother good-night in the following fashion: I applied my mouth to hers with all the suction power I could muster in my prepubescent frame, and I began to rotate my mouth against hers in a precise, almost scientific manner. When my mother was, at least in my opinion, good and kissed, and would stay that way for quite some time, I turned and I looked at my audience, as if to say: "You could be next."

All that kept me from breaking the fourth wall at that moment was my mother, who said:

"Where did you learn to kiss like that?"

"On TV," I answered.

"Well, you're doing it all wrong, hon. You got to open your mouth. Like this."

I opened my mouth. I leaned forward. And, yes, I did kiss my mother good-night in the way she so obviously wanted me to. As I did, a small voice in the back of my head warned: "What do you think you're doing? Now you've gone and fucked your life up but good."

And I was happy.

This was the first time I realized *I had a life*. Something of my own to fuck up. And I felt powerful. Like the most powerful thing I could imagine, which at that time was a waitress at Howard Johnson's on a Sunday morning, seeing that room full of the interminably ravenous and thinking: "I know what to do."

As I made out with Mom, I heard a small sound. Like a door closing and locking behind me. I knew I would never get back to that place where I imagined I was safe.

And, yes, I knew what I was doing was wrong.

But I was surrounded by people who were suffocating under the burden of *a normal life*. I knew I'd rather be wrong than safe. I guess I was at that age when most girls start looking for shelter from the storm.

But I started looking for the storm.

(*Once more the performer transforms into the professor
to announce:*)

Number Three:
"I Was Forced to Participate in Performance Art
As a Condition of My Parole."

I wasn't actually in jail, though I desperately wanted to be. Anywhere my family wasn't. So when my mother asked me if I realized what I had done to Lynne Colbert in the back of our garage was a crime, I said: "Yes."

Then she asked me if I realized that people in this country went to jail every day for what I had done to this young girl, and I said: "So what."

Every day my mother would confront me with a list of my crimes and misdemeanors. I had, for example, told my little sister that she was adopted, that her real name was Gertrude, and that no one was going to buy her a Christmas present. I had broken a branch off the ornamental cherry tree and gone over to the neighbor's freshly poured cement driveway, where I created a little bas-relief, depicting, if I recall correctly, the history of bullfighting. In Michigan.

I believe it was my first triptych.

And every day my mother would try to get me to admit how bad I was. I would always plead innocent. But after I had Lynne in the garage, I cracked. I surrendered to my essentially criminal nature. I knew I never could be good enough to please my mother, so maybe I could be good at being bad. I resolved I would go from bad to worse as soon as it could be arranged.

But my eager confession didn't seem to please my mother. I guess I had robbed her of the joy of interrogation, and those long, lonely hours before she would start to burn dinner just stretched out empty before her.

She asked me to consider the particularly heinous nature of my crime. I knew she was just stalling. But I thought about it because I liked thinking about it. What I had done is I had taken Lynne Colbert, my sometimes best friend and often worst enemy, out behind the Buick, and I had persuaded her to let me give her a little . . . haircut. Lynne Colbert was widely believed to be the most beautiful girl in my elementary school.

But that was *before*.

Before I got out my father's toenail clippers and started hacking away at those long, blonde curls. As I hacked, I persuaded her that (a) she didn't look hideous, and (b) her mother would not beat the shit out of her when I was finished.

And . . . she believed me!

I couldn't believe she believed me! Any more than I'm sure that Jim Jones couldn't believe it when people started drinking that Kool-Aid! I channeled the spirit of my first lesbian role model—Paul Lynde. Particularly Paul Lynde as he was manifest in that seminal piece of queer cinema *Bye, Bye, Birdie*. His spirit sneered through me that day in the garage.

I said: "Kids."

I did not consider myself a kid.

I walked among them but was not of them.

When confronted by my mother, I liked to imagine a big prison devoted to people whose crimes are merely aesthetic. In particular, I liked to envision a big holding tank filled with bad hair stylists. Of course, I was too middle everything to be sent to anything as lively as prison. But I was expected to participate in the nearest equivalent for someone of my *milieu*.

Community theater.

I was under psychiatric orders to work on a production of *The Sound of Music*. This wasn't just any production, oh, no. This was a production under the direction of the most renowned thespians in the entire Thumb region of Michigan. She'd won *kudos* for her previous season's one-woman *Man of La Mancha*.

I wasn't allowed to act. Instead, I was expected to work on the set crew. I was entirely responsible for the Alps. The Alps are pretty damn important in *The Sound of Music*. You got no Alps, you got no music. I was also expected, during the run of the show, to lower a microphone during "Edelweiss" so the Von Trapp children could be plainly heard making that touching homage to those little fascist flowers.

Opening night.

By some fluke, I've managed to get the Alps up on their hind legs. I lower the microphone on cue. But one of the Von Trapp children has another idea. Instead of belting out "Edelweiss," he pivots and farts. Into the microphone.

I have no idea how many of you, if any, have experienced, first-hand, the sheer destructive power of amplified flatulence. But let me assure you, it's nothing to sneeze at. The one thing we had in Saginaw was a damn good sound system.

Pandemonium broke out, praise the Lord. The first thing to go were the Alps. You'd think I'd be upset because they were *my* Alps, after all. But I was delighted. Because all of a sudden you could look backstage and see:

The nuns and the Nazis were the same people!

It was just a question of costumes and phony accents.

Finally the play made sense.

I thought: "This is what I want to do with the rest of my life!"

(*Lights fade to a softer, more romantic level.*)

I've never been what you'd call a morning person.

I'm the kind of person who wakes up so stunned by sleep I can't remember my own name. But now it's starting to become my favorite time of the day.

The difference? It's *her.*

Now I get to watch *her* slide out of the sheets into the new day. Her legs—they're always longest in the morning. I've never known anyone who could get so naked before! She's not in any hurry to do anything about that nakedness. Even though she wears the same thing every day. It's a little present she gives to me, this time. Her standing, back to me, light coming through the palm trees, running over her swimmer's shoulders like river water poured through cupped hands.

That's the moment I remember who I am.

That's the moment I come back to the body I thought I'd lost to my father.

Then she swings around to face me, and Jesus! I'm blinded.

Whatta set of knockers!

Now I know why they call them headlights. Until I started going out with her I never realized: *tits can be a source of light!*

I know there's people who get uneasy when I start talking about my girlfriend's tits. Hooters. Knockers. Winnebagos! I know there's readers who'd be more comfortable if I described my girlfriend's mammalian characteristics as "breastssss."

But I can't do that. She doesn't have breastssss. Thank God! Breastsss are what those ladies have. They like to take their breasts off and hang them up in the closet, where they harden in the dark.

The only good they do them is that they keep all their lady clothes smelling like they just got back from a car trip to Florida.

You know who ladies are, don't you?

Ladies are the people who will not let my girlfriend use the public ladies room, thinking she's not a woman. But are they going to let her into the men's room? Nope. Because they don't think she's a man, either.

If she's not a woman and she's not a man, what in the hell is she?

Once I asked my father what fire was, a liquid, a gas, or a solid, and he said it wasn't any of those things. Fire isn't a thing; it's what happens to things. A force of nature. That's what he called it.

Well, maybe that's what she is. A force of nature. I'll tell you something: *she is something that happened to me.*

But even a force of nature has got to pull a look together.

In the morning, certain decisions have got to be made. So out of the drawers she pulls Jockey shorts . . . not Jockey for Her. The *real* McCoy. And a white cotton T-shirt and a pair of secondhand jeans worn white from the sweat and strain of a stranger's body. A man's body.

Men's clothes. That's all she ever wears.

But putting on these men's clothes doesn't erase her woman's body. In fact, it almost makes it worse. And I'll tell you why. Her tits. They are just *relentless.* The way they just keep pushing through the white cotton like a pair of groundhogs drilling through the February snow to capture their own shadows!

She doesn't even own a bra. Once I asked her why, and she said she didn't believe in them! Like it's not an article of clothing, like it's some kind of prayer. As if strapping on the Maidenform were like saying the Pledge of Allegiance.

I asked her if she worried about her tits falling. She said, "No." She figured that was my job. To catch her tits.

I can be a hard worker!

I'm not particularly known for it, but I can be. So every day I just do my job. I do what I can to start a little landslide in the tit department, and then I scoop them up, using my hands, my mouth, my pussy, whatever's handy.

And every day she gets dressed in the same way. Wearing the same thing, like it was some kind of uniform. Like she's going to war. I guess we are going to war. But sometimes, in the morning, I think we're going to win.

In front of the Ukrainian meat market she pulls me to her, wraps her arms around me, her hands on my ass like the lucky claws at Coney Island, clamping tight and lifting up, and then I'm a candy necklace, a ring flashing secret messages. Gives me a slow deliberate kiss, her body bending over mine like I am a knot she is carefully untying. With her tongue.

Behind us, in the window of the market, a blue and gold sign announces "We're Free!" in two languages. We stay deep in the kiss, as though the sign applied to us as well. And for a moment I'm so happy, I could be Ukrainian.

Then a man whips out of the store. In his arms he's cradling a newborn baby ham. But passing us he names us, he calls us: "*Shameless!*"

Could be that this is the sort of man who thinks anyone, gay— straight, or ambidextrous—kissing in public is shameless. My father's like that. He hates what he calls "displays," meaning that hearts should stay tucked in the pants, hidden, not hung like fat sausages in the greasy public window.

Or it could be that this is the sort of man who thinks that just the *thought* of me loving another woman, even if I never act on it, is a shameless act.

I don't know what sort of man this is. But I wish what he said were true.

I wish I had no shame.

Maybe there are shameless queers. But I know that I'm not one of them, and neither is my girlfriend. I know that buried deep in our bodies is the shrapnel of memory dripping a poison called shame.

But we're the lucky ones. There's not enough shame in us to kill us. Just enough to feel when it rains.

Sure, I've been the cause of tears, lies, and a congressional investigation, but at least no one has tried to cure me. Yet. No one has said kaddish over my still living body while the dead went unclaimed.

I know other queers so riddled by memory that everything they touch becomes a weapon. I have seen shame work its backward alchemy overnight. I've seen people who've gone to bed perfectly respectable bull daggers, only to wake up the next morning claiming to be somebody's wife, a stray Republican, their own mother.

What my girlfriend and I are good at is acting shameless.

In order to pull off this act we've had to perfect two different ways to kiss. The first way is: kissing like there's no tomorrow. At least no Jesse Helms, no Brandon Teena, no AIDS epidemic. Not in our tomorrow.

And we also know how to kiss as if there were no past. She's an expert at shutting out what she has to, so she can do what she wants to. Nothing in the way she swaggers down the street tells the story of how she was shut out that night she came home, sixteen years old, hair cut off, wearing a bow tie, and a new name.

Threatened to do it for months. She'd been dragging around that Jill Johnston book for years. Nobody should have been surprised.

But now she comes home to find the door locked.

A mistake.

That's what she thinks at first, but when the key always hidden under the flowerpot is missing, she looks up. Sees her brother's watching her from inside the dark house that was, until a few minutes ago, her home.

This is a fairy tale, right?

This is the moment the fairy gets her special powers. These are the powers granted to everybody who gets locked out, to everybody waiting outside in the flower bed. It's the power to see into the future. She knows, in the future, there will be other doors locked when they see her coming. She knows that someday this door will swing open again. She'll sit in their chairs and eat their food, she'll sleep in their beds, but she'll do it the way a ghost visits a past life. She'll call this place "the house I used to live in." She won't call it home again.

And her brother? He'll have his special power, too. This is the power granted to everybody who holds a key, to everybody waiting on the inside of the locked door. It's the power to have his thoughts climb inside her head and become her thoughts. Meaning: she will begin to see herself the way he sees her. Watch: Her white clothes will turn silver in the moonlight. She'll imagine she's a silver stake driven into the heart of her mother's garden.

So that's why she doesn't go next door to see if the neighbor has a key. That's why she doesn't pound on the door of her own home and demand to be let inside: she doesn't think she belongs inside. A hole has opened inside her. All of a sudden, a deep hole filling up with the cold water of shame.

This is how she spent the first night of her life as a lesbian: courting sleep in the backseat of a stranger's Buick. As a kid, this is what she wanted. She always wanted to be the outlaw, the desperado, the guy in the black hat. She never wanted any part of *a normal life*. And now she's got her wish.

But where is the rest of the dream?

Where's the getaway car, the chest of gold, the secret hide-out, where are all the other outlaws?

Do I censor myself? Every day.

Because the truth is, I would rather have the man with the ham see us as brazen, would rather not have him see any of my pain, 'cause I know how he would use it against me, against us, would call our pain proof of the illness he imagines we're carrying, when all it proves is:

There is a war going on.
All of us have been hit.
Some of us worse than others.

(*Pause.*)

Don't you hate it when people ask you why you are what you are?

As if you had any idea? All I know is I am a woman who loves another woman who most people think is a man, and that once when we were in San Diego together, okay?

We checked into the best motel, the Hanalei. Polynesian from the word go. Outside a pink neon sign announces: A Taste of Aloha.

You can taste it before you even check in.

There's Styrofoam Easter Island heads everywhere. The bed's a volcano. Every night there's a luau. It's free, it's gratis. So of course we go. And I love the way they slip those pink plastic leis over your head. I just love that! I love the thought of those Day-Glo flowers blooming long after Jesse Helms is gone.

I hope.

I look out on the AstroTurf. Kids chasing each other around. Folks sipping mai-tais and piña coladas out of plastic pineapples. They've got a helluva show at the Hanalei. Hula dancers. Fire eaters. A Don Ho impersonator that's much better than the real Don Ho! Nobody cares it's not the real Polynesia. It's all the Polynesia they could take! It's the one we invented.

During "Tiny Bubbles," she starts kissing me. Everybody's looking at us. But you can only see what you want to see. And what these folks want to see is not a couple of dykes making out at their luau.

So that's not what they see. They start translating us into their reality. What they think they're seeing is Matt Dillon making out with a young Julie Andrews. A young Julie Andrews. Before *Victor/Victoria*.

I don't mind. I'm not in the closet! I'm so far out of the closet that I've fallen out of the frame entirely. They don't have any words for us, so they can't see us, so we're safe, right?

I get confused.

I forget that invisibility does not ensure safety. We're not safe. We're never safe, we're just. . . .

You tell me.

THE END

Conclusion

O ne morning I found myself reading the *New York Review of Books*. I am not the sort of person who reads this sort of magazine; I am the sort of person who shuns magazines without photographs. I am not particularly proud of the fact that my sense of current events has been shaped more by the *Weekly World News* than by the *Nation*, but that's just who I am. However, before I have my first cup of coffee in the morning, it's easy for me to forget who I am. So one fateful A.M., as I skimmed over reviews of books no one I know would ever read of their own volition, I came across an excerpt from Robert Hughes's *Culture of Complaint*, which asserted that Karen Finley and I represented everything that was wrong with American art today.

I folded up the paper and scooted out of the coffeeshop, having reached my target heart rate without the aid of caffeine. Who was this Robert Hughes guy anyway, and what had I ever done to him? I figured he must be a relative. That would it explain it; the bulk of my hate mail comes from my own family.

As I walked up Avenue A, I tried to take in what Hughes had said about me. Tried and failed; it was just too *big*. Oh, sure, I'd been paid similar compliments in the past. God knows I had been mentioned frequently enough on the floor of the Senate by Jesse Helms, who had once dubbed me "a garbage artist." And I had grown used to the way the religious right would use attacks on artists like myself as a kind of bake sale to raise money for their other hobbies like shooting abortion doctors.

Oh, I could go on and count all my citations and awards! But in all these other instances I'd been part of a much larger group. Republicans of the Helms persuasion had accused me of being only one of the many things that are wrong with this country; I was forced to share this distinction with all the other members of the cultural elite: queer filmmakers, welfare queens, rap artists, femi-Nazis, environmental terrorists, undocumented workers, and tenured radicals. I'm sure I'm overlooking many others in this Who's Who of What's Wrong with America, but the point is, I've always had plenty of company.

Now there were only two of us to take on the job of representing everything that's wrong with this country. I'm honored but must confess I'm feeling a wee bit overwhelmed by the enormity of the task Mr. Hughes has given me. Even with Karen's very capable help, I'm not sure I can adequately represent *everything* that's wrong with this country. I don't want to appear ungrateful, but after all it's quite a big country, and Karen and I are just two white girls from the Midwest.

We need help. I haven't asked Karen how she feels about this, so I'm speaking just for myself here. Maybe she feels up to representing her half of what's wrong, but I frankly do not. Mr. Hughes's and Senator Helms's nightmares are huge, and I'm quite certain there're plenty of parts for everyone who wants one. And they are good parts, too. *We all get to be the villains.*

I'm sure many of you out there want to try out but are scared. Maybe you've never been in a show before. You don't feel up to playing a role in a national drama. But I have some news for you. Good or bad news depending on your points of view. If you're reading this book, there's a good chance you're already playing some kind of part in Jesse Helms's or Robert Hughes's nightmares. You may find you've been cast without even knowing about it. So you're in it whether or not you want to be. Up to this point, it's pretty much been their show. They've been writing the script and directing their action. But we can interrupt their show at any point. We can break character and start acting out our own plots. I think you'll find it easier to perform acts of resistance than you think. I have a hunch you're a natural.

Acknowledgments

There's no such thing as a solo theater piece and I don't want to ignore the women and men behind the curtain. I can't thank my agent, Malaga Baldi, enough for holding my hand while I transcribed the scripts off the cocktail napkins on which they were originally written. I am also grateful that whenever I got stuck Jim Moser, my editor, could tell whether what I needed was a push or a pull.

I got invaluable help shaping this book, and particularly the introduction, from many friends including: Lenora Champagne, Jeff Escoffier, Stephen Druckman, Charles Wilmoth, Patty Sullivan, Bia Lowe, Carla Kirkwood, Minnie Bruce Pratt, Phranc, Ellie Covan, Helen Eisenbach, Madeline Olnek, Tim Miller, David Roman, David Cale, and Esther Newton.

A list of everyone who worked on my shows would include almost everyone who passed through WOW, but there are a few whose help was especially important: Kate Stafford, Karen Crumley, Donna Evans, Dona Ann McAdams, Sharon Jane Smith, Lynn Hayes, Chris Vlasek, Gail Freund, Maureen Angelos, Lois Weaver, Peggy Shaw, Alina Troyano, and Lori E. Seid. I'm also grateful for these friendships which have encouraged and challenged me in the last fifteen years: Tim Miller, Eileen Clancy, Signe Hammer, David Cale, Richard Elovich, Daniel Wolf, Jackie Gares, Sarah Lindsay, Janie Geiser, Dan Hurlin, David Roman, Nina Mankin, Cathy Simmons, Kate Bornstein,

Laura Flanders, Elizabeth Streb, Ann Carlson, Mary Ellen Strom, Eleanor Savage, Jan Rothschild, David Harrison, Kestutis Nakas, Jayne Wenger, and Trudy Hughes.

I want to acknowledge the presenters who have continued to support my work, even when to do so has meant funding cuts or death threats, particularly Kristy Edmunds of PICA, Vicki Wolff at Sushi Gallery, Joan Lipkin of That Uppity Theater Company, The American Torture Theater, Ed Cardoni of Hallwalls, Will Wilkins at R.A.W., Loris Bradley of Diverseworks, and Ellie Covan of Dixon Place. Also I'm grateful to all the staff of Performance Space 122 and Highways for giving me a chance to develop new work.

Of course, as a lesbian, I owe the most to my cat, Velveeta, and my fiancée, Esther Newton, not necessarily in that order.